TRAPPED

TAZ BROWN

authorHOUSE

AuthorHouse™
1663 Liberty Drive
Bloomington, IN 47403
www.authorhouse.com
Phone: 1 (800) 839-8640

© 2019 Taz Brown. All rights reserved.

No part of this book may be reproduced, stored in a retrieval system, or transmitted by any means without the written permission of the author.

Published by AuthorHouse 08/20/2019

ISBN: 978-1-7283-1918-6 (sc)
ISBN: 978-1-7283-1919-3 (hc)
ISBN: 978-1-7283-1930-8 (e)

Print information available on the last page.

Any people depicted in stock imagery provided by Getty Images are models, and such images are being used for illustrative purposes only. Certain stock imagery © Getty Images.

This book is printed on acid-free paper.

Because of the dynamic nature of the Internet, any web addresses or links contained in this book may have changed since publication and may no longer be valid. The views expressed in this work are solely those of the author and do not necessarily reflect the views of the publisher, and the publisher hereby disclaims any responsibility for them.

PROLOGUE

A 15 YEAR OLD BOY walks down an empty street in the dark of night. The only light that aided the boy's sight was the bright full moon. The boy had on a dark red hoodie and brown khaki pants. His hands were in his front pockets.

It had been a cold night. The breaths of the boy came out as puffs of smoke. The street that the boy was walking down was surrounded by the huge woods that had the chirping sound of crickets that kept the boy from feeling alone.

As the boy journeyed on to his destination, two bright beaming lights came from behind him. The lights got closer and the sound of an engine grew louder and louder. The boy turned around to see a big red truck following him. The truck pulled to the side of the boy and the boy stopped and so did the truck.

"Need a ride?" a deep voice came from the truck. The boy couldn't see the face of the driver.

"No, I'm good." the boy answered and continued walking. The car slowly started driving next to the boy.

"Where you headed?" the voice asked the boy.

"I'm not suppose to be talking to strangers." the boy said.

"How far is your house?" the voice asked.

"How do you know I'm goin home?" the boy was confused. He stopped walking and the truck stopped moving as well.

The driver stepped out of the truck and calmly closed the door. The boy didn't know what was going on. The figure that stepped out of the truck was large but the boy still couldn't see the person's face due to the bright lights from the truck. The person walked to the boy and he swung an object at the boy's head. The boy fell to the ground hard and tried crawling away but he couldn't. The person slammed the object on the boy's head again and the boy was knocked unconscious.

The person picked up the boy's body and dragged him into the passenger seat of the truck. The person got back into the truck and started his engine and drove down the empty street.

CHAPTER 1

Today is October 20th and it is my little brother's birthday. I wanted to get him a camera, but I don't have to do that because he is dead. He committed suicide last December. He would have been fifteen years old, a year younger than me. His name was Caleb.

It weighed on me for a couple of months, but i began to accept my brother's passing. My older sister was not there to know about his death, she was in California at the time. She got a flight back home as soon as possible when she was told the news.

My dad was never around, so when we tried to reach him, he wasn't available.

My mom was the only one who had been deeply affected about the death. She had went into a deep state of depression and became a totally different person. She would start to drink large amounts of alcohol and would sleep with a guy every night and she would leave the house in the middle of the night and I was always scared that she would never come back but she would later return in the morning. She had been released of her depression when she met Albert and he has been a tremendous help to our family and I'm glad he is here.

I walk down the hallways of high school with my best friends, Rachel and Luke. Luke has been my best friend since elementary school and he was there for me when Caleb had died. Luke is like a brother to me and i don't know how life would be without him.

"So," Luke jumped in front of us walking backwards, "There is a party at Ryan's tomorrow and he wants Rachel to come and I asked if it was okay if all of us went and he said sure and I asked if Kenzie was going to be there and guess what?" Luke had a huge grin on his face.

"What?" I tried to act like I didn't know. I have a crush on Kenzie. I think she doesn't like me but there is a rumor that is spreading that she has a thing for me and I've been waiting for a chance to talk to her about it.

"She's gonna be there!" Luke punched my arm. "I also heard that she might have a thing for you too."

"Luke," Rachel stopped at her locker, "Why would you say that?"

"That Kenzie might have a thing for Chris?" Luke leaned against the locker next to Rachel's.

"No." Rachel opened her locker switching out her books. She shut the locker and we continued to walk to our class. "Why would you say that we're gonna be there? I don't want to go to a party with Ryan.

"He's a dick." I interrupted her. "We know, but just do it for us please. I really like Kenzie and this could be my shot." I put my hands together and begged to her.

"And I really don't like Ryan." Rachel glared at me. "Can't you guys just go by yourselves? I'm sure he'll let you guys in."

"Ryan likes *you*, Rach." Luke tried to persuade Rachel. "He wants you and I think you should give him a chance. Yeah, he can be a dick sometimes but he might not be that way with you. Also, he won't let us in without you."

"I'll think about it, but don't get your hopes high." Rachel said as we made it to our class. We sat down in separate seats and the bell rang.

After school was over, I had to drop off Rachel at her house, so I drove my car and we talked all the way. I met Rachel in the 9th grade and we had become friends at a party and she walked me home after. She is a real good friend and she is very pretty too. She always plays with her hair when she speaks to me and she bites her lip when she forgets something and I think it's kind of cute. She always greets me every morning with those, almost heavenly like, green eyes. Rachel is a beautiful person, but I could never see us being together and I hope she feels the same way too.

"I've decided I'm going," Rachel reluctantly said. "I'm not doing it for you but I'm doing it because I want to have fun."

"Yay!" I smiled still keeping my eyes on the road. "Thank ya, Rach. I love ya." I always say that to make her smile.

"Yeah, love you too." She made a fake mean face and then gently smiled. "I have a question that I've been wanting to ask you lately."

"Go for it." I grabbed my water bottle and drank a little bit of water.

"How come you don't hang out with a lot of black people?" Rachel leaned against the window.

"Huh?" I became confused and started to think maybe I misheard something.

"Like, why don't you like black girls?" Rachel asked. "You don't hang out with a lot of black people and you have two best friends that are white."

"Um," I began to think about the question. "I like all races, Rachel. It doesn't matter the race, it's the personality. Why do you ask?"

"Just wanted to know." Rachel leaned her head back and closed her eyes. "I'm gonna take a nap."

Rachel brought up a good question about me not hanging with black people. I never really thought of it and now that she brings it up, I can't stop thinking about it. I honestly think that maybe it's because I wasn't really a person who hung out with black people. I don't think I really know a specific answer to that question.

CHAPTER 2

I PARK MY CAR IN the driveway of my Mom's house and walk inside. In the kitchen, I see my sister, Joanna, cooking.

"Joanna?" I asked dropping my book bag on the floor.

"Chris." Joanna turned around and smiled at me and threw her hands out running towards me and squeezing me tight. When she released, we both laughed. "How are you, bud?"

"I'm doing fine." I had a huge grin on my face. "How are you?"

"I'm good," She turned around and went back to the stove to turn it off.

"What are you doing here?" I questioned.

"I came to visit for the weekend." Joanna answered. "Wanted to see how my Mom and little brother are doing." She smiled.

"What are you making?" I asked. "It smells good."

"Hot dogs." Joanna laughed. "You thought I was actually making something?"

"No," I chuckled as i picked up my bag, starting towards the stairs. "I'm gonna do some homework." I said continuing up the stairs.

"Alright." Joanna responded.

I walked into my room and sat down at my desk. I got out my book that i had to read and it was called, Moby Dick by Herman Melville. I read and annotated the first few pages and then got bored with it.

I got my phone out and turned on to see a text message from Kenzie that said to call her. I got excited and began to call. After three rings, she picked up.

"Hey," I got up from my chair and started pacing around the room.

"Hey," Kenzie had such a soft voice that it made me want to listen to her all day.

"So," I started to fidget with my hair. "You wanted me to call you."

"Yep," Kenzie sounded a little nervous and I became nervous for some reason as well. "There is a rumor spreading that I like you."

"Yeah," I became a little excited thinking that she was gonna say that she actually liked me.

"I wanted to tell you," She went silent for a moment. "I don't like you like that, Chris."

"Oh," I tried to play it cool but really I wanted to scream in frustration. I was silent for a moment. "Why? I mean okay. I didn't like you like that either. I like someone else, dude." I cursed myself out in my mind.

"Oh," Kenzie sighed in relief. "That's good. Anyways, I'll see you at the party tomorrow. Bye."

"Alright bye." I hung up and threw my phone at my bed.

"So, how was your day, Chris?" Albert asked me as he took a bite out of his hotdog.

"It was fine." I really wanted to say that I hated today but I didn't want to cause anything. "Mom, I'm going to a party with Luke and Rachel, is that okay with you?"

"Sure, but don't do anything stupid." My mom got up from the table and cleaned her plate. "Are you walking to the party or driving?"

"Most likely driving. It's at Ryan's house. Why?" I got up and grabbed Albert's plate and Joanna's plate and cleaned them.

"Because," My mom grabbed a rag and cleaned the table. "I need my car tomorrow and Albert is gonna be out of town and Joanna is gonna be out most of the day and I need the car to go run some errands. So, tell Luke to pick you up in the morning for school."

"Alright," I put the plates in the dish washer and closed it. I walked into the living room and sat next to Joanna to watch tv.

"Then, she said '*I don't like you like that,*' and I just said I was okay with it and i said DUDE!" I shouted in rage in the car with Luke.

"DUDE, that sucks." Luke parked his car in the parking lot of the school. "Why would you say that?"

"I don't know!" I opened the door and grabbed my bag and slammed the door.

"There are other girls to like." Luke tried to cheer me up.

"Yeah, that's true." I said as we walked into the school. "But is there other Kenzie's?"

"Probably not," Luke stopped at a vending machine in the hallway and put a dollar in. "But there is a Rachel." He turned around and smiled.

"You're funny." I sarcastically said as I stuck my middle finger up at him and when he got his drink we continued our conversation and walked towards our classroom.

"I'm just saying maybe you guys are meant to be with each other."

Luke actually sounded serious and I began to think why he would think that and then I ignored it.

"You really think that?" I asked as we sat down at our desks.

"A little," Luke took out his notebook and so did I. "She seems to not like anyone else and she always hangs out with you and me but would rather hang with you. So, either she likes you or maybe she thinks you're gay and she wants a gay friend." Luke laughed as his girlfriend, Emma, walked into the classroom. They shared a kiss with each other and smiled at each other.

"Hey Chris." Emma waved to me and smiled.

"Hey." I waved back to her, smiling too.

"You going to the party?" Emma asked me as she took out her text book and opened it to the assigned page number.

"Yeah. Are you?" I asked as Rachel came into the room with a face full of anger and sat right next to me without saying anything. She took out her textbook and turned to the assigned page number too and started to do the work that was given. Luke, Emma, and I just stared at her.

"Hey, Rach?" Luke walked over to her and kneeled beside her desk. "I don't want to ask if you're okay because you're obviously not, but are you okay?"

"Also," I walked over to her too and kneeled in front of her desk. "Don't say nothing is wrong because we know something's wrong, so tell us what's the matter."

"My brother," Rachel looked up from her work to me still full of anger and then she started to soften and sighed as she answered us reluctantly. "I'm tired of cleaning up his mistakes and hiding everything from my parents about him. He said he would stop doing drugs and then he goes right back to them, he says that he'll stop involving me in the problems and then, somehow, I'm always in the middle of it. He says he will stop and then he doesn't."

"So, did he do something to you?" Luke asked as Emma came over to comfort Rachel.

"Last night," Rachel started to get teary eyed. "He came home late and he was drunk, like usual. He told me not to tell my parents and I said I wouldn't. Then, a while later, I called my parents and told them that Jared wasn't doing so well and they called him and told him that they're gonna kick him out if he doesn't get his shit together. They got a flight back home this weekend. When he found out, he told me I was a bitch and then he freaking slapped me." Rachel wiped a tear away.

"Aw, Rach," I placed my hand on her back and started to rub in a circular motion. "I'm sorry about that—"

"Don't." Rachel looked at me for a moment, then she looked back at her desk. "I'll be fine." Then the bell rang.

"Good morning everyone," The teacher came in and we got ready to begin class.

Luke was driving and Rachel was in the passenger's seat on her phone while I was in the middle of the backseat reading the old text messages that Kenzie sent me. It was dark outside and we were heading to Ryan's house party.

"Dang it. I need some gas." Luke glanced at his speedometer. Luckily there was a gas station near us. Luke pulled in and parked his car by the gas pump.

"I'm gonna grab a drink," Rachel opened her door and looked at me as she was getting out. "You coming?"

"Yeah, I gotta pee." I got up from my seat and Rachel let the seat down letting me out.

As Rachel and I were walking to the store, I glanced to my right to see a large man with a blue cap staring at me. His eyes were brownish and they looked welcoming but at the same time intimidating. He looked as if he was in his mid 40s at least but his bushy brown beard made him look a little older and he looked like he had been through some rough times. He quickly looked away after I glanced at him and he went back to occupying his gas.

"You know him?" Rachel opened the door.

"Nope." I shook my head as I walked through the doors.

Luke banged on the door to Ryan's house. We could hear loud music being played and it sounded muffled. We waited for a couple of seconds, then the door swung open. Emma was revealed to us and she had a beer bottle in her hand.

"Hey, babe," Emma's words sounded slurred. She drunkenly moved to Luke and grabbed his arm and yanked him inside. "I want to show you something." She pulled him through the crowd of teens dancing and talking all the way upstairs. Before the both of them vanished, Luke glanced back at Rachel and I, then he disappeared into the crowd on the second floor.

"Well," Rachel nudged me in the rib. "Looks like it's just you and me, bud." I gave her a gentle smile and she flinched as soon as Ryan wrapped his arms around her waist.

"Hey, Rach," Ryan rested his chin on Rachel's shoulder. He was obviously drunk too. "I've been looking all over for you. Now I've found you and it's like we're meant for each—"

"No," Rachel awkwardly removed herself from Ryan's grip. "No. Nope. I'm dating somebody."

"Who?" Ryan took a sip out of his beer can.

"Chris," Rachel locked her hand in my hand and raised it up in front of Ryan's face. "I'm so sorry dude. Thanks for the invite to the party though. Really appreciate it. Have a good time." Rachel awkwardly grinned and Ryan shrugged and walked away.

"Why the hell did you do that?" I asked her as she released her hand from mine.

"I told you," Rachel leaned against the wall behind her. "I don't like Ryan like that."

"But now everyone is gonna think we're dating." I leaned against the door behind me.

"Then we fake break-up tomorrow in school." Rachel smiled at me. "Lighten up Chris. This is a party, not a funeral. Now let's go have some fun." Rachel gripped my arm and took me through the crowd of sweaty, bad breathed teenagers. She took me upstairs and she opened a door and yanked me into a room full of smoke and it smelled like weed.

"Hey!" One voice sounded. I couldn't tell who it was because it was filled with smoke. "It's our girl, Rachel!" The voice cheered and was followed by multiple sounds of people shouting in the room.

"Hey guys," Rachel released her grip from my arm. "This is my friend, Chris."

"Hi," I waved to the voices hidden in the smoke.

"Wanna try some?" Rachel smirked at me.

"Are all girls confusing," I let out a cough followed by smoke coming out of my mouth. "Or is it just Kenzie because I thought we had a thing and she was flirting and I was flirting and—"

"Woah there buddy," Rachel took the blunt from me and smoked it. "My answer is that all girls are confusing. Sometimes we don't know how to react when a guy tells us that he likes us."

"Yeah dude," One of the stoners said. "Girls are confusing and we will never understand them."

"So, I need to stop worrying about Kenzie," I rested my head on Rachel's shoulder. "Or should i keep trying to go after her?"

"Do what you gotta do bro," Another stoner released smoke from their mouth.

"I'm gonna go down stairs and grab some food," I pushed myself up and headed for the door.

"Wait," Rachel stood up and joined me. "We'll be back. Don't smoke all the weed."

As soon as i opened the door, Kenzie was standing in front of the door with a can of beer in her hand. I just stood there like a statue and she was just smiling at me.

"Hey, it's Kenzie," Rachel smiled.

"Hey Rachel," Kenzie's voice sounded so soothing even when she was drunk.

"How are you?" I said as I became more comfortable.

"I'm alright," Kenzie walked past me and went straight towards a stoner. She took the joint from him and smoked it. "But I'll feel great as soon as this hits me."

"Well," Rachel wrapped her arm around mine. "Chris and I are going to grab something to eat. We'll be back in a moment."

"Yeah, I'm hungry." I smiled at Kenzie awkwardly.

"Come on," Rachel pulled my arm.

"Hold on," I released my arm from Rachel's grip and turned around to say something to Kenzie. "Why would you say that, Kenzie?"

"What," Kenzie looked confused. "Why would I say what?"

"Don't act like you don't remember," I sat down in front of her. "Yesterday, you said, *'You don't like me like that.'* You don't remember saying that?"

"Chris, you're high," Rachel grabbed my arm. "Let's go eat."

"No," I pulled away from her grip. "I want to tell her how i feel."

"Chris," Rachel tried once again to take me out the room. "Come on, bud."

"You don't like me like that, Kenzie?" I asked her rhetorically. "Is it because I'm not strong enough for you? Is it because I'm not hot enough for you? Is it because you don't like black boys? Is it because I'm bla—"

"No," Kenzie coughed and smoke came out of her mouth. "No. That is not the reason. None of those are the reason, Chris."

"Then what is it, Kenzie?" I sounded very calm but was very angry. "Tell me why you don't like me because I really like you."

"I don't like you because," Kenzie scooted in closer and sighed. "Chris, I want you to be with some one who will never break your heart. I want you to be able to trust them. I'm not trustworthy and I'm not ready for a relationship right now. I really think you're an amazing guy but I don't think—"

"It's okay," I stood up and looked down at her. "I mean it's not okay. I've been rejected so many times and I thought that you were gonna be the one girl who would like me. I have liked you for the longest and I thought you liked me too. You led me on and played with my emotions. You—"

"No, Chris!" Kenzie stood up quickly. "I didn't mean to lead you on. I was just being myself. Chris, I like you but not in the way that you want me to. I want to—"

"Let's go, Rachel," I walked out of the room with Rachel.

"You hungry?" Rachel asked trying to get my mind off of Kenzie.

"No," I walked down the stairs with her. "I just want to go home. I don't feel good. Can you drive?"

"Yeah," Rachel sounded hesitant. "Let's go find Luke."

"I'm never talking to Kenzie again." I said to Rachel

"Kenzie, I'm sorry for what i said to you at the party." I was leaving her a voicemail. "I'm a jerk for making you look like the bad guy. Please just call me back."

I sat in the passenger seat of Luke's car while Rachel was driving. Luke was passed out in the backseat. We couldn't let him drive due to the fact that he was really drunk.

"I thought you said that you were never gonna talk to her again, Chris." Rachel glanced at me quickly trying to keep her eyes on the road.

"I know," I leaned my head on the window. "Do you think she's gonna be mad at me at school? Should i write her a card or something? I feel really bad."

"Stop," Rachel continued looking at the road. "Kenzie has a rep at school, Chris. I used to be friends with her. She was nice but she slept with every guy that she met. I'm surprised that she didn't try anything with you."

"So," I said lifting my head of the window. "What are you trying to say."

"Nothing." Rachel smiled. "I'm just trying to make you hate her so you stop talking about her."

"It's not funny, Rach." I leaned my head on the window again.

"Chris," Rachel looked at me and then looked back at the road. "You can't keep your attention on one girl because in the end they might hurt you."

"But I really thought that she liked me." I leaned my head on the head rest.

"You're going to experience that in life," Rachel said. "You just have to wait and be patient."

"Stop the car!" Luke woke up. "I gotta puke. Please, Rach."

"Okay," Rachel pulled the car over to the side of the road next to the woods. The road was empty surrounded by large trees. I hate going down this road because there is nothing but just scary trees and a road.

"Thank you," Luke opened the door quickly and fell out. He gagged then released the vomit onto the grass. It was too dark to see him vomit but i could hear Luke moaning after vomiting.

"You good?" Rachel leaned on the back of the car.

"Does it look like that, Rachel!" Luke yelled as I heard him vomit even more and groan in pain.

"Why did you drink so much?" I checked my phone to see what time it was. I got a text from Kenzie saying that she'll talk to me tomorrow. I became excited as I put my phone in my pocket.

"Was that her?" Rachel sounded a little jealous.

"Yeah," I walked up to her and leaned on the car next to her. I heard Luke vomit again and it was followed by another groan. "She wants me to talk to her tomorrow. I know that you said that I need to stop—"

"Don't listen to me," Rachel rested her head on my shoulder. "I just don't want you to get hurt.

"Thanks, Rach." I said.

"Alright," Luke stood up wiping his mouth. "I think I'm done puking." Luke opened the door to the backseat of the car and hopped in giving us the signal to get back in the car.

Rachel got in the driver's seat and I sat in the passenger seat. Rachel pressed her foot on the gas pedal when the car moved just a little I looked up to see blinding lights speed in smashing the side of the car. I heard Rachel scream as the car flipped down the small hill where we stopped the car. I tried to yell as the car rolled down the hill violently. I felt a sharp pain on the back of my head and then everything went black.

CHAPTER 3

Everything was black. All I saw was black. I started to wonder if I was blind then I started to panic but didn't make any sound. I began to frighten myself remembering the car crash assuming it led to my supposed blindness.

"Chris," Luke's voice was a miracle to me knowing I wasn't alone.

"Luke!" I screamed in relief but I was also terrified thinking that I was blind. "I can't see, Luke. Luke, I can't see! Pleas—"

"Chris!" Luke hissed at me as if he was trying to make me lower my voice. "It's just a blindfold. Take it off."

I took the blindfold off as Luke instructed. I felt so relieved to see Luke standing above me. I looked around to see where I was. The floor was covered in carpet of a red velvety color. There were wooden walls that surrounded us in the small room. There was one bed in the corner right next to where Luke was standing. Rachel was laying peacefully in the bed. She had a bandage on her forehead with a small amount of blood seeping through it.

"I put her on the bed," Luke sat next to me on the carpet and leaned on the wooden wall behind him. "But I didn't put that bandage on her." Luke sounded as if he was worried. "I'm so confused on what happened. All i remember is—"

"Wait," I looked at a wooden door that blended in with the wooden walls around it but the small key hole gave the door away. I got up and walked up to the door placing my hands on it.

"Woah," Luke walked up next to me and stared at the door. "I didn't even see that. I've been looking for a way out of here but I couldn't find anything."

I looked at him trying to figure out everything. "How long you been awake?"

"I've been awake for at least ten minutes," Luke released his eyes from the wooden door to look at me. "I remember the car hitting us."

"Then what happened after that?" I asked walking back to where I was sitting before.

"I woke up," Luke continued on. "I woke up and found myself in here. I saw you and Rachel on the floor and I put Rach on the bed. I started to try and find a way out of here but I couldn't. Then I heard footsteps walking back and forth but didn't know where it was coming from."

I was confused. I started to think that maybe someone took us in and was trying to help us. "Maybe someone is trying to help us. Help us recover or something."

"If they were trying to help us," Luke rhetorically asked. "Then why would they take my keys and phone?"

I checked my pockets to discover that my phone was not in any of my pockets. I walked to Rachel to check if her phone was in any of her pockets.

"Huh?" Rachel woke up gently. "Chris," She touched the bandage on her forehead. "Shit." Rachel winced in pain.

"Don't touch it, Rach," I gently pulled her hand away from her wound. "You can see fine, right?"

"Yes," Rachel sat up.

"Can you walk?" Luke asked still standing by the door.

Rachel stood up and walked towards Luke. "Yep." Rachel turned around to look at me. "Where are we?"

"That's what we are trying to figure out," Luke walked to the bed and sat. "Do you remember anything, Rach?"

"I remember screaming and hitting my forehead hard," Rachel sat down next to Luke. "Do you guys remember anything?" She looked at Luke then to me.

"All I remember was that I saw a truck or something hit the side of the car," I tried to remember what else happened but nothing resurrected from the accident. "I remember the car flipping and then everything went black."

"So what the hell are we doing here?" Rachel stood up and looked at the door that blended in with the wooden walls. "There's a door?" She walked up to it searching for the door to see if she could find an opening. Then, Rachel started to bang on the door. "Hey! Hello!"

"Stop!" Luke ran to Rachel and pulled her away from the door. "Are you insane!"

"What's wrong with you, Luke?" Rachel released her arm violently from Luke's grip.

"You don't know who's out there, Rach!" Luke hissed at Rachel. "That could be a freaking—"

Luke was interrupted by footsteps that sounded like a giant stomping closer and closer to the door. Then, there was a sound at the door and the door shook just a little. It was followed by a sound of keys that seemed to be unlocking the wooden door. Luke and Rachel ran behind me and we all started to become nervous. I could tell that they were afraid because Rachel gripped my arm hard and I could hear Luke's breathing start to get faster.

The door opened slowly followed by a long creaking sound. Then there was a voice that sounded almost deep and raspy. "Put the blindfolds on." Then, the person shut the door and I could hear keys rattle followed by a click showing that the door was locked. I didn't hear the person walk away.

"What do we do?" Rachel whispered very silently.

"Put the blindfolds on," I walked to where i woke up and picked up my blindfold.

"Are you serious?" Luke looked at me as if I said something odd. "Are you dumb or something?"

"Look," I walked up to Luke and talked as low as possible. "We don't know what they are capable of. They could have a weapon or something. We just need to follow the commands so that we don't get hurt." I picked up Rachel's blindfold and handed it to her. "Just do what they say."

"Whatever," Luke picked his blindfold off the floor. "Are we suppose to tell them that we are ready to come out?"

"Yeah, sure," I wrapped the blindfold around my forehead and so did Rachel and Luke. "Everything's gonna be okay." Rachel nodded and pulled the blindfold down to her eyes.

"Luke," I readied my blindfold to pull down to my eyes. "Don't do anything stupid."

Luke reluctantly nodded and pulled the blindfold down to his eyes. I took a deep breath and pulled the blindfold down to my eyes.

"Chris," Rachel whispered.

"Don't worry, Rach," I whispered back and searched for her hand. When I reached it, I locked her hand in mine and squeezed it tightly but gently. "Are you guys ready?"

"Yes," Luke said very quietly.

"Mhm," Rachel squeezed my hand tightly.

"Alright!" I yelled out so the person could hear us. "We got our blindfolds on. What do we do now!"

"Sit down on the floor," The person sounded calm which made me unsettled. "And I'm gonna come in there. Don't try any type of shit that will piss me off because I have a gun and I will use it if I have to."

My heart dropped when he said that. Rachel's hand gripped my hand so tight that it felt as if I lost circulation. I didn't say anything to anyone and I sat down as quick as possible still holding on to Rachel's hand pulling her down to the ground with me.

"Luke," I whispered as low as possible. "Please sit down."

"We're on the ground," Luke sounded oddly calm. "Now what."

"I said I was gonna come in," The person unlocked the door followed by a long creaking sound. I heard the person's footsteps get louder as they came closer to us. Then, they stopped and I knew that they were standing in front of us. "Now stand up."

I stood up as soon as he said it. Rachel's hand still in mine stood up next to me. I could hear Luke get up as well.

"I'm taking the girl first," The person's voice was very deep and they sounded like a man that was southern. "Then, I'll come back and get you boys next."

My heart rate increased dramatically. Rachel's grip tightened. What was he going to do to her? Was he gonna kill her and then us next? My brain became overwhelmed, I started sweating, my mouth was dry, and I felt so helpless and I didn't know what to do.

"Come on," The man grabbed my hand making me jump and pulled it from Rachel's.

"Chris," Rachel's voice sounded as if she had lost her voice. I could hear her and the man's footsteps get farther and farther away then it was followed by the door shutting.

"Luke," I pulled my blindfold off to see him taking his off as well. "What is he going to do to her?" I whispered.

"Shit," Luke had tears slide down his cheeks. He took a deep breath. "We gotta do something, Chris. We gotta get the hell out of here."

"How are we gonna do that if he has Rach?" I hissed at him.

"I don't know!" Luke hissed back aggressively. "Stop asking me questions. You just told me to not do anything stupid."

"Escaping with Rachel is not stupid," I began to argue with Luke. "I thought he was going to help us or something. We can't just leave without her." Then we heard footsteps getting closer to our area. Luke pulled his blindfold to his eyes quickly and I pulled mine down as well. The door opened and the heavy footsteps got closer to us.

"Alright, you're next." The man said as he put his hand on my shoulder squeezing it softly. He pushed me a little as he put his other hand on my shoulder. "Walk." I nervously started walking in the direction his hands turned me in. Then, he took both hands off of my shoulders and I could hear him close the door then locking it. He put his hands on my shoulders again and turned me to the right. It seemed as if we were walking down a hallway. I could hear the creaking sound of the wood on the floor as each foot of ours stepped. He then turned me to the left and we kept going until I bumped into what felt like a table.

"Sorry," I didn't mean to say anything but it just slipped out.

"Not your fault," The man took his hands off of me and sat me down in a chair. "You do have a blindfold on." He untied the blindfold and gently removed it.

When he took the blindfold off, I was sitting at the end of a long, rectangular, wooden table. I looked to my right to see an empty chair then to my left to see Rachel staring at me with red, watery eyes.

"I'll be back," The man walked away from behind me. I didn't even get a chance to look at him.

For a second, I started to think that maybe the man was really trying to help us but I quickly got rid of that thought because why would anyone blindfold someone and lock them in a room with a door without a knob? Even if he is trying to help us, I couldn't let my guard down.

"Chris," Rachel wiped a tear from her eye. "What the hell is happening?"

"I don't know," I wanted to give her an answer but I really didn't know. I observed the area, which had no windows for some reason. The room had wooden walls, wooden floors, and an open doorway which I assumed lead to the kitchen. I turned around to see another open doorway that I guess me and Rachel came from.

"I can't do this," Rachel got up from her seat. "I don't feel right about this. We don't know what is happening and we don't know him. We're leaving. I don't care if he is trying to help us, we don't know him."

"Rachel," I lowered my voice to let her know to keep it down. "I know we don't know him but we can't just leave. We don't know where the hell we are at. Maybe he might be trying to help us or something."

"I don't give a shit!" Rachel hissed. "The guy has a gun. No one who is trying to help someone says they're going to shoot you if you try some shit. You're acting like a dumbass."

"Shut the hell up!" I stood up from my seat. "You just said he had a gun and you think that leaving is a good idea, Rach?"

Then there was the sound of the door closing. I quickly sat down at the table and so did Rachel.

Moments later, Luke and the man came in. I still didn't see the man's face but only the back of his head until he sat Luke down, I saw the side of his face. He looked so familiar but I couldn't really tell if I knew him or not.

"Alright," The man removed the blindfold off of Luke's eyes. "Time for breakfast." The man went into the doorway that I assume led to the kitchen.

Luke looked at me and mouthed the words, *"What the hell."* I just stared at Luke not knowing how to answer. I could hear, in the kitchen, bowls being taken out of a pantry followed by the noise of what sounded like cereal being poured into the bowls. Next, I could make out the sound of a refrigerator door being opened and then closed, then opened again and then closed again.

"You guys like cereal?" The man walked back into the room carrying two bowls placing one in front of Luke and one in front of me. He walked back into the kitchen and came back with two more bowls putting the bowl in front of Rachel and placing one in front of an empty seat that was across from where I sat. He sat down at the empty seat and just stared at us. The man was big but not fat, he was just muscular but not too muscular, like a bear. He had a brownish beard with gray hairs that covered the bottom half of his face, like a lumberjack. His eyes looked almost tired but for some odd reason they seemed young and innocent. His hair was the same color as his beard but with more gray hairs. He wore a plain, white shirt that had some dark spots as if he was playing in dirt. He wore blue torn up jeans from what I remembered when he was standing up. Then that's when it clicked. I remembered him from the gas station.

"Oh," The man caught himself as if he realized something then flashed a smile. "I didn't even introduce myself. That was rude of me. My name is—"

"I saw you at the gas station." I interrupted the man. Shit. I'm such a dumbass. I wasn't suppose to say that out loud. "I'm sorry, I've just seen you before." The man's smile faded then disappeared and he just stared at me with those, now, unnerving, terrifying eyes. I could hear my heart beat get louder and faster. My mouth turned dry, my blood became cold and my body was as still as a statue. There was a long, uncomfortable silence and the man just stared at me while I just sat there looking at him with frightened eyes. He was like a wolf preying on a helpless animal.

"My name is Logan," Logan smiled again and closed his eyes then sighed. "I am a nice and friendly guy. But, if any of you interrupt me like that again, you will be punished." He opened his eyes and looked at Luke. "Do you understand?" Luke hesitated for a second and then nodded his head. Then Logan looked at Rachel and smiled a little more. "Do you understand?" Rachel nodded as well. Then he turned to me and his smile faded away. "Do you understand?"

"Yes, Sir." I nodded oddly.

"Okay," Logan took a bite of his cereal. He looked at us as if we were stupid while the milk ran down his beard. "Eat your cereal before it gets soggy."

Me and Rachel quickly ate our cereal after his demand but when I looked up at Luke, he was just staring at Logan who didn't even notice that Luke was staring at him. Then, Logan looked up after eating another bite of his cereal. Luke quickly began eating his cereal.

"Why were you staring at me?" Logan sat straight.

"Huh," Luke stopped eating his cereal and acted as if he didn't do anything. "What do you mean?" Luke sounded sarcastic but I felt like he was being serious.

"Don't act like you don't know what you were just doing," Logan clenched both of his fists. I looked at Rachel and she was staring at Logan's fists.

"I'm the one acting like I don't know what I'm doing?" Luke glared at Logan. "Do you know that you're kidnapping us? Do you know that you threatened us? Do you know that—" Luke flinched as Logan interrupted him

"NO!" Logan roared as he slammed his fists on the table breathing ferociously. Then, he closed his eyes and took a couple of deep breaths. Out of nowhere he started counting. "1....2.....3......4," one deep breath, "5...6....7....8," another deep breath followed by the tapping of his fingers rhythmically on the table. "9……10." Logan let out a sigh opening his eyes. Luke just stared at Logan in fear.

"Why are you still staring at me?" Logan's tone sounded like a growl of some violent, brutal, terrifying monster.

"Just let us go." Rachel tried to look at Logan but just couldn't seem to keep her eyes on him.

"Darling," Logan stood up and walked to Rachel. He gently stroked her hair then he put both of his hands on her cheeks lifting her face forcing her eyes to meet his. "Look at me. Look at me when ya say something." Rachel tried removing his grip from her face but she couldn't and his grip just got tighter making her face turn red.

That's when, out of nowhere, Luke slammed a chair on Logan's back, causing Logan to collapse to the ground. I was just stuck there in fear, witnessing what Luke had just done and I didn't know what to do until Luke snapped me out of my petrification.

"Come on!" Luke had Rachel's arm and he yanked me out of the chair making me fall to the ground. I stood up and followed Luke and Rachel out of the room into the hallway. "There." Luke pointed at a door that, from what I saw, had four locks on it and I was hoping it was just my imagination.

"Shit!" I yelled as we got close to the door finding out that there was four locks on the large door. The worst thing about these locks is that they needed keys and we didn't have any keys.

"What the hell!" Luke complained violently as he banged on the door and trying to kick it open.

"You little shit!" Logan's voice exploded with rage as I could hear him knocking things down trying to get up.

I tried to look for a key holder around the area but there was literally nothing on these wooden walls except for a stupid clock and two pictures but then there was something on the wall that was in the middle of the pictures and clock. It was a large brown gun that just sat there as if God was giving me and my friends a chance of escaping this beast. I grabbed the gun, which was actually pretty light, and aimed it down the hallway as I could hear Logan groan in frustration as his footsteps got louder and closer to our territory.

"Chris?" Rachel looked at the gun in confusion.

Luke tiredly stopped banging on the door and turned around to see me with the gun. "Where the hell did that come from?"

Logan revealed his giant, monstrous body down the hallway. I could see a small gun gripped in his right hand but he didn't have it raised to aim at us. He just stood there and breathed heavily like a tired lion. Then he took a step forward to us.

"Back the hell up!" I screeched trying to sound tough making sure I was ready to shoot but I had never held a gun in my life, so I probably looked very awkward trying to threaten him with a gun. "We just wanna leave, okay. There doesn't have to be any problems."

He smirked and took a couple steps closer to us.

"Please!" My eyes started to become watery blurring my vision of him a little. I didn't want to shoot him and I didn't want to kill him. I had to give him one last warning. "If you come any closer, I will shoot you!"

He took a deep breath and flashed that same smile that he had flashed at the table. Then he walked closer and closer and didn't stop.

"Shoot him!" Luke screamed in panic.

"Chris!" Rachel cried out.

"Shoot him, Chris!" Luke continued to scream. "Shoot him!"

Logan got closer and closer.

"CHRIS!" Rachel's cry for my name made me make my decision. I felt the adrenaline travel through my body putting my finger on the trigger, glaring at Logan's monstrous eyes. It was time to get out of here, call the cops and go home to my family and we would never have to worry, my mom would't have to worry, Rachel and Luke wouldn't have to worry. I would shoot this beast and get my friends out of here. I pulled the trigger.

Then, nothing happened.

"There's no bullets." Logan said.

CHAPTER 4

"Just let us leave." I begged still aiming the gun at him as if there were actually bullets in it. "We just wanna get out of here, alright."

"Yeah," Rachel's voice sounded calm. "We won't tell anyone what you did and we won't call the police."

"Just give us the keys," Luke tried to compromise with Logan. "And we will leave and all this would have never happened."

"Yeah?" Logan seemed to be persuaded. "So, if I let you leave none of this would have never happened?"

"Yep," Luke seemed to become more relaxed believing that we were gonna get out of this place. I didn't believe that Logan was convinced that easily.

"Nope," Logan's tone became deep. He raised his gun up and directed it at me. "Put the gun down and walk back into the dining room and sit your ass down!"

"Please—" I attempted to speak.

"Do as I say!" Logan's shout made me jump. "SIT YOUR ASS DOWN AT THE TABLE AND DON'T SAY ANOTHER GODDAMN WORD!" I see his grip on the pistol get tighter, seeing the veins on his fist bulge out as if they were gonna explode.

I did as he said placing the gun slowly on the wooden floor. I walked towards him slowly feeling like I was walking to my death. Every step was followed by a long, drawn out, groan of the wooden floor. As I got closer to him my hands started to tremble and my body felt so cold. I tried to not look at him as I passed. He kept the gun aimed at my head. Once I made it to the dining room, I sat down in the seat I had sat in before, taking a breath and just sitting there staring at my bowl of soggy cereal.

"Hurry up!" Logan snapped. I didn't turn around to see who it was who walked in but eventually it was revealed to be Rachel who sat in her original seat. She didn't even look at me. She just stared at her cereal. She was horrified and I couldn't do anything about it. I couldn't save her and Luke from Logan's wrath. I could've gotten them out of here.

I could hear the footsteps of Luke and Logan behind me as they made their way into the dining room. As they passed me, I saw Logan had the gun aimed as it was touching the back of Luke's head. I was hoping that Luke wouldn't do anything stupid.

Luke sat down at his seat in silence and looked at me with a plain face. I didn't know if he was plotting something else on Logan or if he was just really terrified and didn't know how to function. Logan stood behind Luke still holding the gun to his head.

"Wow." Logan lowered his gun and tucked it behind in his pants. He sighed as he looked down to see the chair that he sat in previously, broken apart. He walked over to where Luke slammed the chair and bent down, picking up a piece of wood, which I assume was one of the legs of the broken chair. He gripped it tight with his hand holding it like he was going to knock somebody out with it. He looked at Luke with a snarl.

"We just want to leave." Luke tried negotiate. I could tell he was afraid of what Logan was going to do next with the piece of wood. Logan held it closer to Luke's face. "We won't tell anyone. Just let them go. You can do whatever you want to me, but just let them leave, please." Luke's face started to become red.

"No," Logan dropped the piece of wood on the floor. "Stand up, boy." Logan stared at Rachel and then at me as Luke slowly stood up. Then, intensely, Logan gripped Luke's collar raising him off his feet. He slammed Luke into the wall. Logan threw him to the floor.

"Stop!" I stood up from my seat. Logan turned his attention to me quickly pulling out his gun aiming it at Luke. "Just stop." He then slowly aimed the gun at me and I didn't care. I just wanted to save Luke. Logan walked towards me. He swung his arm, whacking me across the face with the gun causing me to fall onto the floor.

"Don't!" Logan roared as he aimed the gun at me. "Don't try any of that shit ever again. Y'all will be some dead sons of bitches if any of you try that shit again!" Logan tucked his gun in his pants and walked over to Luke grabbing a blindfold, wrapping it around Luke's eyes. "Stand up." Luke did as he was told. Logan and Luke walked off out of the room leaving Rachel and I.

I stared at Rachel and she stared at me. We were not getting out of this place.

We were back in the room that we woke up in.

"What the hell is wrong with you." Rachel said as she observed the bruise on my cheek.

"I'm okay." I looked over at Luke. He was sitting on the opposite side of the room just staring at the door. "Luke, are you good?"

"No," Luke continued to stare at the door. "He slammed me against a wall. He threatened us with a gun." He turned his attention towards me and Rachel. "Why is he doing this?"

"I don't know." I stood up walking towards the door.

"Do you think the cops are looking for us?" Rachel asked. "They have to be looking for us."

"Yeah," I turned around to face Rachel.

"Do you think they will ever find us?" Luke asked. "Because I don't think they will."

"Why?" Rachel looked at Luke.

"Did you not see the dining room or the door we tried to escape out of?" Luke stood up. "There were no fucking windows or anything."

"What do you mean?" I tried to understand what he was getting at.

"When do dining rooms have no windows?" Luke hissed at me and Rachel.

"Okay," Rachel also seemed to not understand what Luke was trying to say. "What are you saying?"

"I'm saying that what if we're in the middle of nowhere." Luke answered. "I'm saying this house is built out of wood and there are no windows. I think he was planning to do this shit."

I didn't know what to say to Luke. His idea seemed crazy, but, it didn't sound wrong.

"You think he planned to kidnap us?" Rachel was confused. "That doesn't make sense."

"I think it does." Luke walked to the bed and sat down. "It makes sense because Chris even said that he saw this guy at the gas station."

"Yeah," I leaned on the door. "But why would he want to take us?"

"You saw him at the gas station," Luke began. "Then we went to the party. Then, we left and then the car accident. Now, we're here."

"He hit us with the car." Rachel looked at Luke. "You think he was following us."

"Yep." Luke stood up. "But why would he want us?"

"We're jumping to conclusions." I thought this was chilling and I didn't want to believe it. "Maybe we got hit by somebody else and he came to help us or something—"

"Chris!" Luke whispered as low as he could walking up to me. "Are you serious right now? Think about it! *You* said that you saw him at the gas station. We woke up here after we got hit and now we're in the house of a kidnapper that you saw at the gas station. That just sounds weird to me."

"You're right," I had to accept that Logan had to be following us and that he was that same guy at the gas station. "I just don't know why he would do this."

"Do you think that he has done this with others?" Rachel became pale.

"I don't know," Luke looked at Rachel. "But he's a psycho. We're getting out of here."

27

"What!" Rachel whispered loudly. "Are you crazy. He has a gun, Luke. We can't do anything unless you wanna die." I could tell Rachel was frightened. She was right about escaping. If we tried to do that; one of us would end up dead.

"She's right, Luke." I tried to convince him. "We should just wait for the cops. Our parents have probably already called them and they're looking for us right now."

"No," Luke didn't care about what I just said. "We need to have a plan for when we go out there again." He paused and noticed that me and Rachel were not going to agree with him. "Listen, the cops are not gonna come anytime soon and we don't know what this maniac is going to do to us before they come."

"But if we try to do any type of shit like that again," Rachel looked at me. "He'll use that gun on us. I would rather play it safe."

"I would rather leave this place as soon as possible, Rachel." Luke argued. "Hoping the cops come is a waste of time and I want us to get home as soon as possible."

"We won't be able to go home if we get shot." I entered into their argument siding with Rachel. "I know you want to get out of here and we all want to get out but we can't do that if we're dead." I walked to the other side of the room to the bed and sat down. "We need to all stay calm and keep it safe and that means we go by his rules."

"You guys are crazy." Luke sat down leaning his head on the wall.

I thought about what Luke's argument when he said *'we don't know what this maniac is gonna do to us.'* Maybe he was right. *We* didn't know what Logan would do to us before the cops come. We also don't know where we're at. *What if the cops can't find us, what if we get killed before they come, what if we never can go home.* All these thoughts were racing through my mind and I became more nervous each time I thought about it. I began to think that Luke was right about leaving this place as soon as possible.

We sat there in the silence for a couple of minutes.

"Never mind," I broke the silence. "Forget everything I just said. We need to get out of here as soon as possible."

"Wait, what?" Rachel was puzzled. "We can't do that. We need to all play it safe. You just said that."

"Well now," I looked at Rachel and then Luke. "I think Luke is right. I would rather at least try to get out of this place before something bad happens to us."

"Alright," Luke stood back up. "We need to think of a plan."

"I think this is stupid." Rachel glared at me. "I don't want to die and I don't want you guys to die."

"I know this is scary." I sat down in front of her putting her hands in mind. "But, if we don't do anything or at least try, then we probably won't ever get out of here."

"Come on, Rach." Luke sat down next to her. "We need each other to get out this place."

"It doesn't look like I have a choice." Rachel was angry and afraid. "So, what's the plan?"

CHAPTER 5

"W̲E NEED TO GRAB a hold of the gun." Luke began. "We gotta get that first then we force him to give us the keys."

"Alright," Rachel was standing in front of the door. She turned around to face us. "How are we gonna get the gun?"

"He has tucked in behind in his pants." I tried to think of a way to get it. "We need to get him to somehow take it out."

"How can we do that?" Luke asked. "We can't do that unless…" Luke paused and looked at me.

"Unless we get him to aim it at one of us." Rachel finished Luke's sentence. "We can't do that. That's just asking for death."

"There is another gun." I tried taking our minds off of the other idea. "The big gun in the hallway. He probably hid it."

"Yeah, we don't know where he put it because we haven't seen the whole house. We've only seen the dining room, the hallway, and this room." Luke continued.

"I saw the kitchen." Rachel came to sit down with us. "My seat in the dining room was facing it."

"What did it look like?" I asked.

"Did it have any doors or openings?" Luke also asked.

"Um," Rachel tried to remember. "I remember it was very small and narrow, like skinny. I didn't see any windows or doors. He doesn't have a pantry. He got the cereal from the top of the refrigerator."

"Then we need to forget the rifle and go back to the pistol." Luke said.

"No, we need the rifle and the pistol." I tried to think of another way to get it. "We know the pistol is in his pants but we don't know where the big gun is if it's not on the wall."

"Does anybody need to pee?" Rachel said out of nowhere.

"What?" Luke and I both asked in confusion.

"We need to be able to find the rifle. There's no bathroom in this room. He's gonna have to let one of us go to the bathroom. One of us could look around the house while one of us distracts him in here and we would threaten him with it and we could force him to give us the keys and the pistol."

"I'll do it." I said feeling my chest get tight.

"Are you sure you want to do that?" Luke looked at me as if I was crazy.

"Chris," Rachel grabbed my hand. "I can do it j—"

"No," I interrupted her. "I'm gonna do it. I've snuck out of my house before and I can do it here. All I need to do is find out where the rifle is?"

"Yes," Rachel said. "But the rifle doesn't have any bullets."

"Son of a bitch!" Luke whispered aloud.

"No, No," I tried to keep everything optimistic. "I can try and find the bullets as well."

"We can't do this," Rachel started to hesitate. "You won't make it."

"I can do this." I tried to keep her thinking positive. "We're getting out of here, Rach." I reassured her.

"When are you going to do this?" Luke asked.

"I'm ready." I answered.

"Okay," Rachel stood up. "What are we gonna do to distract him?" She looked at Luke for an answer.

"We need to just keep him in this room." Luke responded. "I'll think of something."

"Alright," I walked up to the door. "Let's hope this works."

"Just be careful." Luke put his hand on my shoulder.

"Make it back and get us out of here." Rachel wrapped her arms around me holding me tight. She released and took a deep breath.

31

I banged on the door. "Hey! I gotta go to the bathroom!" I waited for a response. I heard his footsteps get closer to the door and I moved back a little.

"All of you put the blindfolds on and sit down on the floor." Logan sounded tired.

I turned back to see Luke and Rachel sitting on the floor already putting on there blindfolds. I grabbed mine off the floor and wrapped it around my eyes then, sat on the floor. "Okay! I'm ready."

I heard the door shake and the keys rattle followed by a drawn out creak from the door opening.

"Which one of you gotta go?" Logan growled.

"Me." I raised my hand.

"Stand up." he demanded. I stood up and he walked behind me putting both his hands on my shoulders. "Walk." I walked and he turned me to my right. He released his hands off my shoulders then he shut the door and I could hear a click which I guess was him locking the door. He put his hands on my shoulders again pushing me a little forcing me to walk. We walked and walked until he turned me to my right again. I heard a door open and he placed his hand on my shoulder pulling me. "You can take the blindfold off."

"Okay." I took the blindfold off to see a small bathroom. There was a shower next to the toilet and the sink was right next to the toilet. It was a pretty small bathroom. I stood over the toilet and looked to my left to see Logan standing there glaring at me. I quickly looked down at the toilet. "Can I close the do—"

"No," Logan cut me off. He leaned on the door and crossed his arm. He then sighed. "You are some ignorant kids."

"What?" I gulped.

"Here, let me refresh your mind" Logan continued. *"One of us needs to look around this house while we distract him"* Logan reached behind him taking out his gun. He didn't aim at me; he just held it at his side. *"We'll threaten him with the rifle and get the keys and get the fuck out of here. He's been following us. He's a psycho; a maniac!"* Logan roared at me.

I didn't know what to do. He knew our whole plan. Shit! He's gonna kill us. "What are you talking about?" I tried to act clueless.

"Shut the hell up!" Logan roared. He stomped towards me and grabbed my neck and threw me to the floor. I felt helpless, this was my death, I was gonna die to him. I quickly got up but was knocked down to the floor again when he swung his fist at my jaw. He got down to the floor on his knees and threw a hard jab to my nose twice causing me to hit the back of my head hard on the wooden floor. Everything felt dizzy and I saw multiple Logans and then he threw another punch. I felt a sharp pain in my nose and I could feel it throbbing.

"Sto-st-stop." I tried to speak but it felt impossible.

He grabbed my collar and picked me but my body went limb and I fell back to the ground but he still had a grip on my collar and he dragged me through a long hallway. I couldn't really see anything but I looked up to see a clock and two pictures and in the middle of it was the rifle. He dropped me on the floor and took out some keys from his pockets and stuck them in the wall with the rifle. Then the wall opened. He threw me in the room.

"Chris!" Rachel's screech hurt my ears.

"Shut the hell up bitch!" Logan yelled. "I'm not a maniac! I'm not a psycho!" He slammed the door and I could hear him lock it.

"What the hell happened?" Luke ran up beside me and so did Rachel. She placed her hand on my face and her other hand in my hand.

"Your nose is bleeding." Rachel's eyes started to become watery.

"I'm fine, Rachel." I tried to make her not feel worried.

"No you're not." she rubbed my hand. "See Luke! This is what I'm talking about!" She screamed at him in anger.

"What!" Luke screamed back. "It was your idea in the first place!"

"Shut the hell up!" she cried. We're not gonna all get out of here if we try to fight. One of us is going to get hurt! Don't you understand that Luke!"

"Fuck you!"

"Fuck you, Luke!"

"Both of you need to shut up." I tried to settle them down. "This is all of our faults. We were stupid to think he wouldn't be listening. Everything we say can be heard by him."

"Well can he hear this," Luke walked towards the door. "You're an asshole! Go to hell you...you piece of shit!" Luke slammed his fists on the door multiple times.

"Stop!" I demanded. "That is not gonna do anything but piss him off even more." I sat up against the wall wincing in pain. "He's strong and we need to all take him down at the same time. We can't be alone."

"He's gonna pay for this." Luke banged on the door one last time. He took a deep breath and walked to the bed then he sat down putting his face in his hands.

"Go talk to him." I whispered to Rachel. She got up from beside me and walked to the bed sitting next to Luke. She placed her hand on his shoulder.

"I'm sorry for yelling at you." Rachel apologized.

"I'm sorry for losing my shit." Luke sighed. He looked at me. "This is my fault. I'm sorry, Chris. I got you into this mess."

"Don't apologize." I wanted to make him feel better. "We didn't think the plan through thoroughly."

"You're right." Rachel sighed taking her hand off of Luke's shoulder.

"You said we should play it safe, right?" Luke looked at Rachel. She nodded. "Then let's play it safe."

"We need to work together and stay together at all times." I said grabbing my blindfold and putting it up to my nose to stop the bleeding. It was so painful that I wanted to cry; but there was no time for that. If we wanted to get out of here, we needed to do it cautiously.

CHAPTER 6

WE SAT IN THE dining room eating lunch in silence. Logan just sat there watching us eat our sandwiches. He looked angry. He didn't even touch his food, he just watched us but he was mostly glaring at me. I couldn't help but glance at him as he glared at me. I took a bite out of my sandwich.

"I'm sorry for breaking your chair." Luke finished eating his sandwich.

"Shut up and eat." Logan turned his attention to Luke.

"But I'm already done eating." Luke was being arrogant.

"Luke," I kicked his leg. "Shut up."

"I *am* sorry." Luke actually was being serious.

"Apology...not accepted." Logan was not having it. He turned his attention to Rachel. He smiled a little. "Boys. Always doing dumb shit like slamming chairs over people's back."

"Why are you doing this?" Rachel was not playing it safe.

"Excuse me?" Logan's smile quickly disappeared into a frown.

"You got any more sandwiches?" Luke tried to change the topic.

"I just want to know why you are being nice to us and feeding us." I could tell Rachel was lying.

"Eat your food." Logan wasn't buying it. He stood up and walked to Luke. "Put your blindfold on." Luke did as he was told and stood up. Him and Logan walked out of the room.

"What was that?" I whispered to Rachel. She didn't answer as she stood up walking away from the table into the kitchen. "Rachel."

"Just keep watch." she whispered loudly.

"What are you looking for." I stood up and peaked my head out to see the hallway. Logan and Luke just made it to the door.

"I got one." Rachel came tip-toeing back into the dining room sitting at her seat. She started to eat her sandwich fast. I tip-toed back to my seat and finished my sandwich. I wonder what she got.

Logan came back into the room and took Rachel out of the room. I sat in the dining room alone. I felt afraid and wanted to be with my friends. I wanted to know what Rachel had retrieved from the kitchen.

Logan walked into the ding room again and sat down at the table. I was confused. I thought he was suppose to put me in the room with Luke and Rachel. He took a bite out of his sandwich.

"I'm sorry for hurting you kid." Logan surprised me. "I'm not a bad guy. It's just that you kids need to respect me in my home." he drank from his cup.

"I'm sorry for disrespecting you." I wasn't sorry.

"Apology…accepted." Logan flashed a quick smile.

I didn't know if he was trying to trick me or something but I wasn't gonna fall for it. I'm not that gullible. I just had to keep playing it safe.

"What did you grab?" I asked Rachel. We were back in the secret room. I was still thinking about Logan apologizing. It was weird to hear him do that. Was he actually sorry?

"I grabbed a knife." she whispered as she pulled it out from her pocket. "We can use it against him the next time we go out there."

"You think a knife is gonna help when he has a gun?" Luke questioned her.

"She did the right thing," I thought that Rachel was smart for grabbing the knife. "At least now we have a weapon."

"Yeah, I guess." Luke collapsed onto the bed. "That's a step closer to getting out of here. Good job, Rachel."

"Thank you." Rachel walked over to Luke putting her arm out to give him the knife. "Take it."

"Why?" Luke sat up.

"Because," Rachel put it in his hands. "I don't know how to use it."

"What makes you think I can use it?"

"Just take it, Luke." Rachel desperately tried to not hold the knife anymore. "I don't want to hold it anymore."

"Fine," Luke stood up and lifted the mattress up a little. "We need to hide it somewhere here just in case he searches us." He whispered as he slid the knife under the mattress.

There was a long silence. We all sat in different places of the room just staring at different things. I thought about my mom. She was probably freaking out about this. I wanted to go home and let her know I was okay. She can't deal with losing another son; she wouldn't be able to live. I hate Logan for taking us. He took us and now my mom is going to go through another hard time. I need to get out of this place. We need to get out of here.

"Do you think he was planning to only take one of us?" Rachel asked out of nowhere.

"I have no idea." I responded. "What makes you say that?"

"Well," Rachel pointed to the bed. "There's only one bed." She analyzed the bed. "I think he's done this to other people."

"How do you get that from staring at a bed?" Luke looked at Rachel in confusion.

"I don't know." Rachel laid on the floor. "I just want to know why he's doing this."

"He's a mental," Luke sat up. "He threw a fit when he heard me call him a psycho. He's insane."

"He apologized to me." I recounted. "It sounded believable but I wasn't falling for it."

"This guy is weird." Luke scolded as he walked to the door. He turned around to face me and Rachel. "You think we could use the knife to open this?" he whispered.

"I don't think so." I whispered back. "He's probably standing outside right now."

"He said sorry?" Rachel went back to what I previously said.

"Yep," I replied. "It was weird. He sounded like he actually meant it.

"Did he say anything else?" she asked.

"He said he doesn't like when people disrespect him," I answered. "I said that I was sorry and he smiled and he was like, *'apology accepted,'* and I didn't know what to do so I just waited for him to finish his sandwich and bring me back here."

"Wow," Rachel was shocked. "Maybe he knows what he's doing is wrong."

"I guess." I wonder if he actually knows what he is doing. "He obviously doesn't want to kill us."

"Yeah," Luke snapped. "But, he obviously wants to beat us up and throw us against walls and break noses."

"Relax, alright." I demanded. "We need to keep our cool and play it safe."

"I'm sorry." Luke apologized. He walked back to the bed and laid down resting his head on the pillow.

"How's your nose?" Rachel asked as she came to comfort me.

"It still hurts like a lot." I said as I touched my nose wincing in pain. "But I'll be okay."

"I should've never thought of that idea." Rachel sighed.

"Stop it." I insisted.

"No," Rachel looked me in my eyes. "I brought up the idea and now you have a broken nose."

"It's fine, Rach." I put my hand on her knee.

"How are you so calm about this?" Rachel rested her head on my shoulder.

"I'm not," I rested my head on the wall. "I'm freaking out on the inside." I closed my eyes and slowly drifted off into a deep sleep.

CHAPTER 7

I was awoken by the banging of a door. Rachel quickly woke up as well removing her head off my shoulder. I quickly stood up and so did Rachel. Luke sat up on the bed and reached his hand in the mattress removing the knife from under it. He tucked it in behind in his pants and stood up beside the bed.

"Are you guys ready for dinner?" Logan mumbled from behind the door.

"Ye-yes." Luke stuttered rubbing his eyes.

"Alright," Logan unlocked the door. "Blindfolds on."

I grabbed my bloody blindfold and wrapped it around my eyes.

"We're ready!" Rachel yelled out.

"Okay." Logan opened the door and put his hands on my shoulders first and walked me to the dining room and took off my blindfold. I sat there in silence waiting for Rachel and Luke to come in.

It smelled nice in the dining room. He must've cooked something really good. It smelled like burgers and fries.

Next, Logan and Rachel came in and sat down at the table and Logan walked out again. Then, he came back with Luke and he sat Luke down at the table. Logan walked out of the room and came back with two plates filled with french fries and burgers. He placed them in front of me and Rachel then he went back into the kitchen and came back with another plate and placed it in front of Luke.

"Thank you." I thanked him as he sat down.

"You're welcome." Logan murmured. "There's some more burgers if you want seconds." He smiled at Luke. Luke nervously smiled back at him.

We sat there eating in silence for a long time. Logan just stared at us just like he did at lunch. The burgers were really good and I wondered if it was because I hadn't really eaten anything except for a couple bites of cereal and a sandwich.

"You're not gonna eat?" Luke asked trying to start a conversation.

"I'm not hungry." Logan leaned back in his chair. "I already ate."

"Thes-these are really good." Rachel complimented Logan. He smiled at her. It made me want to punch him in the teeth. He kidnaps us and acts like nothing has happened. But, i need to maintain myself and make sure we get out of here alive.

"So," Luke pointed out to Logan's chair. "Did you get a new chair?"

"No," Logan answered. "I had a spare one in the back. I actually built this one."

"Oh," Luke finished his burger. "So you know how to build?"

"Yep." he replied. "It's a talent that I have. I built the house and most of the things in it. I built that room that you guys are staying in as well."

"Oh, wow." Luke glanced at me and then looked down at his plate as he ate a couple of fries. "I, um, th-that's impressive. I'm impressed." I could tell Luke was nervous. I looked at Rachel and I also could tell that she was nervous.

"How long did it take you?" I had to make sure there was no silence that filled the room.

"It took me about six months, I think." Logan looked at Luke's empty plate. "You want some more?"

"Uh," Luke thought for a moment. "Yeah…sure." He handed Logan the plate. Logan grabbed his plate and got up walking into the kitchen. We all looked at each other. Rachel was shocked and so was Luke. I was afraid. He built this place and it proves that this guy *was* planning this shit.

Logan came back with the plate and placed it in front of Luke. Luke took a bite out of his burger.

"Thank you." Luke swallowed.

"How long has this place been built?" I asked wanting to know more about Logan.

"Um," Logan sat down in his chair. "I think it's been up for bout eight years."

What the hell?, I thought to myself. Has he done this to others? Has he kidnapped other kids? What happened to them? Did he kill them?

"I'm tired." Luke yawned as he stretched his arms out trying to break the silence.

"Alright," Logan stood up and waited for Luke to put on his blindfold. They both walked out of the room leaving me and Rachel.

"What the hell." Rachel whispered as she quickly emptied her plate.

"I know." I agreed.

Logan came back and waited for Rachel and she put her blindfold on and they both walked out. While they were gone, I sat there in silence. I stuffed the burger and fries in my mouth and finished eating. I put on my blindfold and heard Logan's footsteps get closer to me. I stood up and he put his hands on my shoulder and walked me to the secret room. He unlocked it.

"Goodnight." He said as he opened the door and gave me a light push. The door shut and I heard him lock the door and walk away. I took off my blindfold and just stared at Luke and Rachel.

"What the hell was that?" Luke spoke as low as possible.

"Eight years!" Rachel hissed. "He's done this to others. He built this room and this house eight years ago."

"We gotta get out of here as soon as possible." I walked over to the bed and sat down leaning against the wall.

"Tomorrow morning," Luke removed the knife from behind his pants. He walked over to the bed and slid it under the mattress. "We're getting the hell out of here. Forget playing it safe."

"We need a plan." I fidgeted with my blindfold. "And we need to talk quietly."

"Well," Luke sat down next to Rachel. "We've got a knife." He made sure to whisper. "We need to stab him with it and grab the pistol and keys."

"We need to make sure he's knocked down." I insisted. "He's huge. You slammed a chair on his back and he still managed to get up."

"Alright," Rachel spoke out. "Then we need two to hold him down while one of us gets the keys and the gun."

"Yeah," Luke looked at Rachel and then at me. "Me and Chris will have to hold him down."

"We're gonna threaten him with the knife?" I asked.

"We're gonna have to. Rachel's gonna grab the things while we keep him down."

"Alright then," I looked at Rachel and Luke. "We've got a plan."

"Yeah," Rachel replied. "We just need to make sure that it works."

"Rachel," Luke put his hand in hers. "You need to grab the things fast. When you grab them run to the door. Me and Chris will keep him down buying some time for you to unlock that door."

"Okay." Rachel nodded nervously.

"Are you sure you can do this Rach?" I wanted to make sure she was okay. I honestly didn't want to do this but it was the only thing that would get us out of this place.

"Yeah, I've got this." Rachel took a deep breath. "We need to work together to get out of here and this will get us out of here."

"What do we do when we get out?" I asked.

"We run and don't look back." Luke looked at me like he was nervous. "This is gonna work." Luke sighed. "We're gonna get out of this place."

CHAPTER 8

Rachel was asleep on the bed. Luke and I were still awake. He had the knife in his hands twirling it as he stared at the door.

"You really think this is gonna work?" he asked.

"No," I replied. "But it's the only thing that might actually work."

Luke went silent for a moment. He looked at me. "I'm scared, Chris." he sighed placing the knife on the floor.

"I am too." I reassured him. I looked over to Rachel. "We all are." I looked back at Luke. "I want to get her out of here. She doesn't deserve this. Both of you don't deserve this."

"You don't either." Luke walked over and sat down next to me. "Do you think you deserve this?"

"I don't know." I picked at a finger nail. "I just think that this is a punishment for me."

"Why?" Luke had a puzzled look.

"Because," I began. "Ever since Caleb died, I've been feeling guilty about not being able to do anything. I feel responsible for him taking his own life." My eyes were beginning to become filled with water. "He just needed someone to talk to. He felt alone and he felt like no one cared." I looked at Luke. "I deserve this because I was being selfish and not looking out for my brother, Luke." I put my face in my hands and sobbed.

"Stop, Chris!" Luke hissed as he pulled me wrapping his arms around me. "This isn't your fault, man. Don't blame yourself. You're not the one that got us into this. No one is to blame here except for that motherfucker out there. He kidnapped us."

I just stayed there in Luke's arms crying for a couple of minutes. Then he patted me on the back.

"Get some sleep, alright." he removed me from his hug and went over to grab the knife and slid it under the mattress. He went to the opposite side of the room and sat down staring at the wall. I laid down on the floor next to the bed and closed my eyes.

I was in a hallway with blue lockers on both sides of the walls. It was bright and it was difficult to fully open my eyes. I knew this hallway; my school. It was filled with emptiness but I could hear different voices coming from behind. It sounded like a crowd of people whispering.

"Chris!" a familiar voice called out to me.

I turned around to see my brother, Caleb. He smiled at me as he walked to me stretching his arms out in front of him and wrapped them around me tightly.

"Caleb?" I was confused. I didn't know what was going on. I wrapped my arms around him sinking my face into his shoulders. It all felt so real but in the back of my mind I knew it wasn't. I didn't let go and kept him in my arms knowing that if I let him go, I would never be able to hold him again.

The lights started to darken. The voices stopped abruptly. It was now silent. I let go of Caleb and noticed that he looked frightened. His eyes started to get watery and tears began to slide down his face.

"Caleb?" I was scared and I tried to grab him but my hand went through him. Then, there was loud stomping coming from behind that got louder and closer. I turned around to check and saw Logan standing at the end of the hallway looking furious. He was running toward us and as he got closer, he got taller and bigger as if he was mutating into some creature. I turned around to alert Caleb.

Caleb stood there, his mouth full of pills that were spewing out uncontrollably. They started to consume the floor and I began to sink into the thousands of pills. I screamed as I sunk deeper and deeper into deadly drugs. I reached my hand out struggling and saw Caleb's face for the last time before the pills devoured me.

I woke up from the nightmare. My heart was pounding and it felt hard to breathe.

After gaining control of my breaths, I propped myself up and backed myself into the wall behind me to rest my back. I rubbed my eyes to adjust to my surroundings. I looked to the bed where Rachel peacefully slept and then looked opposite from her to see Luke passed out on the floor.

I just sat there for a while not knowing what else to do other than sleep. Sleep was not an option at this moment after what I just dreamt. I couldn't stop thinking about it and it haunted me to think of him and Logan.

I got up and stretched. I decided to look around the small, square room to see if there was anything else in it. I was hoping to find a secret door or something but Logan isn't that simple. I pressed my hands against the walls to at least see if anything would open but there was nothing.

I looked under the bed out of curiosity. There was nothing. But then I saw something under the bed that looked like a hole in the mattress. I stuck my hand in and blindly searched hoping that there was something interesting in it.

My hand found some type of leathery thing. I grasped for it and it was pushed away from me. I tried to reach further for it but I barely touched it with my fingertip. I pulled my hand out and sat up sighed wondering what it was.

I turned around to look around to see if I could do anything to grab what I was looking for. I looked at Luke and remembered that he had slid the knife under the mattress. I turned back and put my hand in between the mattress and pulled the knife out.

I laid back down on the floor and stuck the knife into the fabric of the mattress and started cutting. I cut and cut until something fell down. It looked like a book. I reached for it and pulled from under the mattress to see that it was not a book but a journal.

I looked at Luke and then Rachel wondering if I should wake them. I looked back down at the journal and decided to open it. I flipped through it and saw that there was writings written in black ink on the first few pages. The rest of the journal was blank. I flipped back to the first page and rubbed my eyes to comprehend the writing.

I began reading.

CHAPTER 9

6/16/16

My name is Connor Underwood. I am 15 years old. It has been a month since I've seen my family. I have been trapped in this room and this man, Logan has kidnapped me and this girl. We have tried everything to get out of here but there is nothing. I have given up on trying to get out of here but the girl hasn't given up. Her name is Annie. She is scared of Logan and I am as well. He hasn't done anything to me but he has done things to Annie. He slaps her and touches her and other things. He seems to be fond of me because he always smiles at me and it creeps me out. He gave me this journal because I told him that I like to write and he wanted to give me something to do when in this room. I hate him for what he has done to Annie and I. I don't know if he knows what he's doing is wrong but he deserves to be punished for this. He told us at dinner that he built this room six years ago. It makes me wonder if he has done this before and how many people has he done this to?

6/18/16

It's been two days since I last wrote in this. Nothing has happened today which was odd. Logan didn't seem happy and he didn't talk to us at the table today. I don't know why I am even writing this journal. I think I write to make sure I don't lose my sanity. Looks like we're not getting out of here anytime soon. Annie hasn't said anything to me today. She's taking a nap right now. So I'm gonna go and I'll write if anything happens.

6/25/16

It's been a while since I have written. There's been a lot that's happened over the past few days. Logan kidnapped another kid. Her name is Julia. The other day she pulled a little stunt that Logan didn't take so well. She threw a plate at Logan's face and it made this huge cut in his forehead and he grabbed her by the neck and slammed her to the ground. I wanted to help her and I decided to get up to interfere but Logan had pushed me against the wall and pointed his gun at me. He looked horrifying with all the blood rushing down his face. I couldn't do anything and I just stood there. He had a gun to my face, what was I supposed to do? That's when Annie jumped in and stabbed Logan with a knife in the back and that's when it happened. Logan turned his attention to her and he had shot Annie in the head. Her body had fallen onto the table and the blood had flowed out of her head onto it. Julia screamed and I was just shocked. Logan looked sad like he didn't mean to shoot her. He started breathing hard and ran to the kitchen and started crying. I was petrified and

I couldn't move. I fell to the ground and I couldn't get the image out of my head. Julia had ran to me and attempted to pick me up and tried to tell me that we had to get out of here but I couldn't move. It was like something was holding me down. Annie was dead and that's when I knew that this man wasn't fucking around and that we needed to leave. I haven't been able to sleep for the past few days and I don't know what to do. Julia has been trying to talk to me about a plan to get out of here but nothing will work. He'll kill us if we try any dumb shit and I'm not trying to die and I don't want Julia to die either. I told her that we need to wait for the cops to come but both us knew we were not getting out of here.

7/4/16

Happy Fourth of July! I hate myself for even writing this. Today was surprisingly fine. We went outside for the first time to shoot fireworks. As we were shooting fireworks, I was looking around and noticed that there were a bunch of trees that surrounded us and in the middle there was a narrow opening that looking like a road leading to the place we were at. We were isolated. I could have gotten away but I was too scared. No one was going to find us. The only way was to try to escape and that shit won't work. Today was kinda nice and Logan had made us a cake and it was good but I still don't like him and I still want to get out of here. I hate Logan for what he has done to us and I want to kill him but I can't do that. If I tried anything, Logan would crush me like a bug and I would die and then Julia would be left alone with this psycho. I'm thinking of ways to get out of here but there is nothing that seems to work in my mind. I just want to go home.

7/10/16

Hey, this is Julia Perron writing in Connor's journal. I don't know why I decided to write in this but Connor hasn't written in it for days. He is sleeping now and I can't fall asleep. Connor's a good guy and he doesn't deserve this bullshit. I want to get him out of here and I'm trying to think of ways to get out of here. I hate Logan and I want him in hell. He's a killer and deserves to die. I'm too scared to do anything to him because the guy is huge. He seems to like Connor and he hates me and that's probably because I won't take shit from him. Connor always follows Logan's orders and I always give him a hard time but recently I have given up on being tough to him. Maybe I need to act like I'm scared to make Logan like me so that I can trick him in order for us to get the hell out of this place. There has been, surprisingly, some good days. Logan has treated us well, not a lot though. On the 4th of July, he made a cake and he took us outside to shoot some fireworks. It was nice but I still hate him and nothing that he can do will make me change my view of him. He is still a killer and an abuser. Annie's family will no longer be able to see her and Logan took her away from them. I miss my family. They're probably worried sick about me. I want to just get back home and see them. I hope they get me and Connor out of here. I'm gonna go and try to fall asleep and I probably won't write in this thing again unless I get bored.

7/12/16

It's me again, Connor. Still stuck in this place. I saw that Julia wrote in this and I think we should start taking turns. I might actually ask Logan for a t.v. because every time we go back to this room, it's boring as hell. Julia and I mostly just talk about stuff and we get to know each other more and more each day. She told me she was raised by a single parent - her dad- and she has two brothers. She told me her mom had died in a car accident. We told each other about how we ended up here in this shit hole. I was walking down the street trying to get home and that's when Logan pulled up next to me in his car and asked me if I needed a ride and I told him no. He didn't care and he knocked me out and I woke up here. Julia had a different, more brutal way of how she got here. She told me that she was driving home after babysitting and her car had broken down. She told me that she thinks that he did something to her car to make it break down because she had seen him before she began babysitting at a nearby gas station. She said that when her car broke down, he had just randomly appeared with his truck and asked if she needed help and she said that she had called her parents and it would be fine. Logan had gotten out of his truck and that's when Julia tried to tell him off and he got a wrench from his truck and hit her twice in the head with it and she woke up here. I never learned how Annie had gotten here. I remember she had told me that she was there two days before me. Logan is a murderer and he needs to be stopped before he does this to anymore kids like us. I don't know how many people he has done this to. I'm gonna go tell Julia my plan that I have been thinking of for the past few days. This one might actually work.

7/21/16

I'm an idiot. I can't do this anymore. I could've saved her. She didn't deserve this. Julia is dead. She didn't even do anything. I told her to do nothing and he killed her instead of me. It was all my fault. She didn't even do anything. I deserved to die for what I did, NOT HER! I got her killed. Logan heard us talking about my plan and he knew we were going to try to get out of here. I told him it was all my plan and he walked over to her and shot her. I don't know what to do. I'm all alone. I'm scared. I just want to go home! HE'S A MANIAC!

7/25/16

I give up. Today I will leave this place one way or another. I will try to escape and if I can't escape the house then I will shoot myself to leave this place for good. I can no longer stay in this place. I will lose my sanity. No one is coming to find me and no one even cares about me anymore. People have forgotten about me. They will never find me So why stay somewhere when I can just take the easy way out. For anyone who is in here, just try your hardest to get the hell out of here. If you are reading this and you get out of here just please show this to my family. My parents and my sister, Dawn. Tell them that I tried to get out and that I love them. I hope to God if you're reading this that you escape from this psycho.

CHAPTER 10

I CLOSED THE JOURNAL. WHAT the hell did I just read. Logan's done this to other kids and he's murdered them. They had families and they had a future and he took that away from them.

I was shocked. My eyes became watery knowing that this was real and that Connor, Annie, and Julia had lost their lives due to this monster. I didn't know what to do. I just sat there with my millions of thoughts. Millions of questions going through my mind. *How many times has he done this? How many kids has he killed? Why is he doing this?*

I started to become terrified at the thought that Logan could kill us at any time. I woke up Luke and Rachel quickly.

"What?" Luke tiredly rose up. He yawned as he rubbed his eyes.

Rachel woke up after him. She sat up in the bed. "What's wrong?"

I showed them the journal. Rachel walked to us and sat down.

"What the hell?" Luke squinted his eyes. "Where'd you find this?"

"Under the bed," I opened it and showed them the writings. "There was a hole under it and I found it. Logan has done this to other kids, not just us."

"Oh my God." Rachel grabbed the book from me flipping through the pages.

"Logan gave this kid named Connor this journal," I continued to tell them about what happened before us. "He wrote in it. There was two other girls that were here with him. They were in here for a month."

53

"What happened to them?" Luke asked as Rachel handed him the journal.

"Logan killed the two girls." I said, feeling frightened by the fact that there was a murderer in this house. "I don't know if he killed Connor or if Connor killed himself. He wrote that he was going to kill himself."

"This happened two years ago." Luke read the dates inside the journal. "How the hell did they know what day it was?"

"I guess Logan told them." I answered. "But that's not important. This plan that we are pulling tomorrow may not work."

"We have to do something." Luke didn't want to give up on the plan. "We can't just stay in here and wait for help to come to us. You see that they were in here for a month. If we just sit here, we could be stuck in this place longer."

"He's right." Rachel agreed with Luke.

"I'm not saying that I want to stay in here," I continued. "I just don't want any of us to die. I think we should wait to carry out this plan."

"Chris." Rachel said. "We need to do this."

"Did you not see what he did to them?" I asked rhetorically. "Rachel, he killed them!" I hissed. "He killed them. I'm not letting either of you die. We just need to be safe about this."

"I'm sorry," Luke stood up. "But I'm not staying in this place any longer. We have a plan and we have to execute it. It's three of us against him. We can do this, Chris."

Rachel put her hand in mine. "I know that I didn't want to do this before but I'm ready now. I'm scared but I'm ready."

"I just don't want to let you guys die." I didn't want to do this plan right away after reading the journal. We could die. I tried again at persuading them to back down from this suicide plan. "There is time that we could use to make a more safer plan."

"There is no safe plan, Chris!" Luke became frustrated. He took a deep breath as he sat back down to level with me. "Do you want to stay in here and rot or do you want to get out of here and see our families and make sure this man doesn't do this to any other kids?"

I didn't answer. He was right. We could just do this plan and hope for the best instead of doing nothing.

"Yeah I understand that there could be consequences," Luke calmed down. "But that's a risk I'm willing to take."

"We have to get out of here, Chris." Rachel implied. "Please don't back down from this."

I thought about it and left them in silence. I stood up and walked to the other side of the room calculating all the possible outcomes of the plan in my mind. "Okay." I turned around to face them. "I'm sorry. I just wanted to keep you guys safe."

"You're right for being scared." Luke said as he stood up. "I'm scared too but I'm not gonna let that keep me waiting for help that's never coming."

I want to make sure that this plan works. I keep thinking of the worst possible outcomes when we carry out this plan. I hope this works and I hope nothing bad happens.

I was the only one awake while Luke and Rachel fell back asleep. There was a loud banging on the door which was Logan. Rachel and Luke rose up quickly. I grabbed the knife and removed it from the mattress. I handed it to Luke and he tucked it behind in his pants.

"Are y'all up?" Logan yelled.

"Yes." Luke responded. As he grabbed his blindfold and wrapped it around his eyes.

I grabbed mine and so did Rachel. She wrapped it around her eyes and took a deep breath. I took a deep breath and wrapped the blindfold around my eyes.

"We're ready!" I yelled out to Logan.

CHAPTER 11

We sat at the table eating pancakes. I looked at Luke and then at Rachel. Luke was eating his pancakes and drinking his water like he had not eaten in days.

"You hungry?" Logan smiled at Luke. "Fast eater. You need some more?"

"Yes. Please." Luke smiled back at him as he swallowed his last piece of pancake. "And please may I have some more water." He drank the last drop of it.

"Alright." Logan got up from the table and made his way into the kitchen. "My pops taught me how to make these pancakes." Logan said from the kitchen

"Well, your dad has made some great pancakes." Luke said in a cheerful voice while looking at me giving the sign that he was ready to carry out the plan.

Rachel kicked me to get my attention. She mouthed something but as soon she was about to finish, Logan walked into the room and she stopped and looked back at her plate.

"How do you like the pancakes?" Logan asked looking at me as he put a few more pancakes on Luke's plate.

"They're delicious." I tried flashing a smile. I saw Luke move his arm behind him and I kicked him shaking my head subtly. I can't believe he was just gonna do it that quick. We need to wait for the right moment and not rush it.

Logan walked back to his seat and sat down. "And how bout you sweetheart?" He grinned at Rachel.

"It's good." Rachel awkwardly smiled at him as she took a bite out of her pancake.

"It's not great?" Logan's grin faded away. I saw his hand start to ball up into a fist.

"My name is Chris." I stopped whatever was about to happen. Logan looked confused and so did Rachel and Luke. "We never told you our names. I'm Chris and that's Rachel and that's Luke."

"Oh," Logan smiled as he remembered. "You're right. I can't believe I forgot to ask." Logan chuckled.

"Yep." Luke joined in laughing. Rachel looked at me and mouthed the words *'thank you'* and quickly joined into the awkward laughter and so did I.

"So, Chris," Logan smiled. "You want some more pancakes?"

"Yeah, sure." I had to say yes in order to carry out this plan. I needed him to feel comfortable with us so that he wouldn't see it coming.

Logan got up from his seat and walked back to the kitchen. I looked at Luke and he looked at me. I nodded to him showing that I was ready. He nodded back as he reached behind him and took out the knife put it at his side. He was ready.

I looked at Rachel and nodded at her and saw that she looked a little nervous but she nodded back.

Logan walked over to me and placed two pancakes on my plate. My heart was pounding and I began to feel weak but I wouldn't let that stop me from carrying out this plan. I smiled at Logan as he walked back to his seat.

Logan sat down and sighed. He flashed another smile. That's when Luke jumped at Logan with the knife and aimed for his neck but missed and stabbed his shoulder. Logan collapsed to the ground. Luke struggled to keep him down on the ground. Logan screamed in pain and anger.

"Chris! Rachel!" Luke yelled for our help.

I quickly got up from my seat and jumped on top of Logan next to Luke and held him down. Rachel came to us and started searching as quickly as possible.

"Hurry up!" Luke yelled at Rachel as we struggled to keep Logan down. He was squirming and using all his power to get up but we managed to keep him down. Luke held the knife in Logan's shoulder and pressed on it to make Logan weak as the pain was too much for him.

"I'm trying, Luke!" Rachel reached behind Logan and I heard the shaking of the keys. "I got em!" Rachel sounded cheerful as she held them up.

"Go Rachel!" Luke screamed at her.

"What about the gun!" Rachel asked.

"Forget it!" Luke screeched. "Go to the door and open it. We'll hold him down! Just go! Go!"

Rachel scrambled to her feet and ran out of the dining room into the hallway.

"Hold him down as hard as you can." Luke demanded as he reached behind Logan.

"What are you doing?" I yelled at Luke. "This wasn't the fucking plan!"

"I know but we gotta get—"

Luke was interrupted by Logan throwing me off of him. I quickly got back on top of him and pressed the knife hard into his shoulder. He winced and screeched in pain as he fell back onto the floor.

"I got it!" Luke had the pistol in his hand. "Get up Chris!"

"Are you sure!" I yelled at him wondering if that was the right thing to do.

"Just get up!" Luke aimed the gun at Logan. I got up quickly and heard Logan groan as he struggled to get up but Luke pointed the gun at Logan's face. "Stay the hell down!"

I stood behind Luke not knowing what to do. Logan stayed on the ground like Luke demanded. He removed the knife from his shoulder slowly and he screamed loudly as he did it. There was blood dripping from the knife and he threw it to the ground. There was an expanding stain of red on his shirt from the wound.

"You little shits!" Logan started to get up but Luke whacked him across the head with the pistol. Logan fell back to the ground and grabbed his forehead. "You piece of shit! You don't know what to—"

"I said stay down!" Luke quickly put his aim back on Logan. "I will use this thing! Grab the knife, Chris!"

I quickly grabbed the knife and held it up in defense just in case.

"Rachel! Are you almost done with those locks!" I yelled as my heart started pounding harder and harder.

"I'm on the third one!" Rachel yelled back.

"Go help her." Luke lowered his tone still focusing on Logan with the gun. "I'll make sure he doesn't get to the door."

"No," I denied his request. "That's stupid. I'm not leaving you alone."

"Just go, Chris!" Luke wasn't going to say it again. "She needs help and I got him down. I'll be fine."

"Luke, don't be a dumbass." I argued with him. "I'm not going to leave you with him."

"She needs help!" Luke said breathing hard. I could tell he was nervous. "I got him, Chris. Just go."

"Look," I tried to persuade him. "It's not time to be a hero."

"Chris, just go!" Luke yelled. "Go help her so we can get the hell out of here."

I became frustrated but he wasn't going to budge. He was right, Rachel did need help and Luke looked like he knew what he was doing with the gun. I reluctantly walked out of the dining room, putting the knife in my pocket. I saw Rachel struggling at the end of the hallway door. I ran to her.

"I can't open the third lock." Rachel said trembling. I could see that her hands were shaking and sweating. She dropped the keys and quickly picked them up and tried the lock again. There were six keys on the holder and I took them from her and tried each key.

"We're gonna get out here, Rach." I said breathing faster than normal. I stuck one of the keys into the lock and turned it and heard a click. It was unlocked. "One more lock!" I yelled to Luke. I continued to find the key to unlock the last lock. It was only six keys, why was it so hard to find the right one?

"Stay down!" I could hear Luke scream from the dining room. "I will shoot you!"

"You won't!" Logan roared as I heard a plate crash onto the floor. I turned around to see what was going on but I quickly turned back to focus.

Then, there was a loud bang. Rachel screamed as it scared us both. It sounded like a gunshot. There was another bang. I heard something collapse to the ground.

"Luke!" I continued focusing on trying the lock. There was no response; it was silent.

"Luke!" Rachel called out as she began walking to the dining room slowly.

I turned back to stop her but I returned my attention back to the lock. Did Luke shoot Logan? Did Logan shoot Luke? The thoughts made me unsettled. So, I stopped trying the lock and ran up to Rachel grabbing her arm.

"Try the last lock." I advised her.

She did as I instructed and rushed back to the door.

"Luke!" I said as I walked slowly to the dining room, afraid of what I might see. My heart began to race as I came up to the opening. "Are you alright?" I wanted him to respond but he didn't. Maybe he was shocked or maybe—

"I didn't mean to." Logan's voice could be heard.

I looked from Logan, who had the gun in his hand, to the floor where I saw him. This wasn't happening. This can't happen. I felt like collapsing to the floor. I felt like I was going to faint.

"I didn't want to—" Logan had tears running down his face.

Luke was on the ground, his chest rising up and down rapidly. He was gasping for air as he reached out to me. There was one bullet hole in his neck and one in his chest. The red liquid began to take over his shirt.

I stumbled to the ground ready to pass out as I crawled to him hoping that this was some type of fucked up dream.

"Lu-L-Luke," I said kneeling beside him pressing my hands on his neck to try and stop the bleeding. The blood was beginning to cover my hands. "Rachel! Get in here!" I cried out to her and heard her rush into the room.

"Luke!" she screamed.

"Come over here." I demanded trying to stay calm. "Put your hand on his chest, okay, where the wound is, alright." I said hoping to stop the bleeding and save my best friend.

"Chris." Luke choked my name out as blood spewed from his mouth. He tried saying some other words but couldn't manage to get them out.

"It's alright, Luke." I said as I moved one of my hands into his hand that was reaching for help. I squeezed it tightly and looked at him in his eyes that started to tear up. The tears slipped from his eyes washing away some of the blood from his mouth. "You're gonna be fine."

I could hear Rachel begin to cry. I looked to her.

"The blood." she said as I could see the blood start to pour out more and more from his chest.

I looked back at Luke as he let out a long breath. His chest slowly deflated and his mouth fell open.

"Luke." I whispered as I felt like I couldn't talk. "Lu-Luke." I began slapping his cheeks to wake him up leaving a bloody handprint on his face.

I began to panic and cry. Tears blinding my view of him.

"No," Rachel cried out to me. "He's not—"

"No!" I didn't want to believe it. I rested my face onto his and just sat there crying. Then, something came over me as I remembered who did this to him. He was standing right behind me. Anger began to to take over my sadness.

I turned around to face him. I got up and took the knife from out of my pocket. I held it up, ready to fight.

"Rachel," I wiped the tears to get a clear view of this monster. "Get behind me." She did so as she cried.

Logan was frozen in shock. He didn't even care that I was about to kill him. He just stood there with the gun at his side as he stared at Luke's lifeless body.

"He had a sister." I told him in a calm voice. "She's nine years old. Her name is Lexi." I gripped the knife tighter. "He had a mom and a father. You took away their only son!" I raised my voice in anger.

"He…he had the gun—" Logan tried to get the words out to make some dumb excuse.

I lunged at him with the knife, screaming as I did it. He grabbed my arm and threw me to the ground. I lost my grip on the knife. He aimed the gun at me, his finger on the trigger.

"Do it!" I begged letting the sadness take over again. "You didn't have a problem before! So why don't you just shoot me! You killed Annie! You killed Julia! You killed Luke! So just kill me! Shoot me!"

"No!" Rachel screeched. "Don't shoot him."

"Get up!" Logan grabbed my hair and yanked me up. He turned around to Rachel pointing the gun at her in his other hand. "Give me the keys."

Rachel gave him the keys with her bloody hand. She looked at me with fear in her eyes. Her face was red and she had tears falling down her cheeks.

Logan dragged me out of the dining room.

"No!" I yelled trying to fight him back. "I'm not leaving him!"

He didn't listen. We made it to a wall where the rifle and two paintings and a clock were placed. He struck the key into a small little hole. He twisted it and there was click. The wall opened. It was a secret door.

It was the room that we had been stuck in. This is where he was hiding us; behind this wall.

He threw me in. He didn't say anything and he walked away. I just sat there not knowing what to do.

He came back with Rachel and threw her in the room with me. She fell on top of me. I held her in my arms as she began to cry even more.

Logan just stood there looking at the floor trying not to make any eye contact. I could see that he had tears in his eyes. He looked at me and then closed the door gently, locking it.

Our plan failed. We were still in this room. We still had to live in this house with a murderer, a monster, a maniac. I lost my best friend; a friend that was like a brother to me after I had lost my real brother. He killed Luke. Logan took away Luke from me, he took him away from Emma, and he took him away from his family.

Luke was dead.

CHAPTER 12

Four days have passed since Luke's death. Logan has been bringing our food to us instead of us going out into the dining room to eat. He doesn't say anything to us and he just opens the door and gives us each a plate of food. He doesn't make any eye contact with us. It feels like he is more afraid of us than we are of him.

We now sit here eating sandwiches and chips for dinner. Rachel sat on the bed and I sat on the floor opposite of the bed. We sat there in silence. We haven't spoken to each other in days. We're both still in shock from this death.

I want to kill him. I want to kill Logan but there's nothing that we can do. There's no hope and there's no plan that will work.

Connor's journal was a sign; a warning. I should've stayed with Luke in that room. I should've been there to jump in front of the bullet or stop Logan from grabbing the gun. I could've stopped it, I could've saved Luke.

Emma's no longer gonna be able to see her boyfriend. Lexi is no longer gonna have an older brother to look up to. Luke's parents aren't gonna be able to raise their only son. Logan took that all away from them.

"I'm sorry." Rachel apologized for some reason.

"For what?" I was confused. I took a bite out of my sandwich.

"It's my fault." Rachel had a tear run down her face. "If I had just been quick enough to unlock those locks, I could—"

"Stop." I cut her off. I walked up to her and sat down with her. "It's not your fault. Don't blame yourself for this. We can't stay in here and just blame ourselves for something out of our control." I paused as my eyes began to fill up with tears. "Logan did this. Luke was trying to protect us…and Logan killed him." I wiped a tear with the back of my hand. "This is his fault. He put us in this place. He kidnapped us and took us from our families and friends. This is all his fault, Rachel. Not ours."

Rachel wrapped her arms around me and rested her head on my shoulder.

That's when we heard the door shake and there was a click. Rachel sat up. The door opened and Logan walked in. He stepped in and closed the door behind him. He stayed on the opposite side of the room from us. He didn't make eye contact with us as he stared at the floor crossing his arms.

"Listen," Logan cleared his throat. "Starting tomorrow, at breakfast, we will eat together in the dining room."

"Okay." I said in a low voice.

"I'm..I'm," Logan was about to say the words. "I'm sorry for—"

"Shut up." I said very calmly. "You don't get to apologize, you bastard. You deserve to—"

"Goodbye." Logan quickly walked to the door and unlocked it opening it and closed it locking it back.

How could he do that? How could he apologize about something that caused many people much pain? He doesn't deserve to apologize for killing Luke.

We sat at the dining room table for breakfast. I now sat in Luke's old seat and Rachel sat in her original seat. I stared at the floor next to me where his life was taken away from him.

"What exactly happened?" I took my gaze off the floor and glared at Logan.

"Wha-" Logan was about to ask.

"What exactly happened when you shot him?" I interrupted him knowing he was going to ask that dumb question. "How did you manage to get the gun from his hands into yours? How did he have the gun and end up getting shot twice by you?" I let my anger engulf me.

"I fought him." Logan explained. "I pushed him to the ground and grabbed the gun. He got up and rushed towards me and I shot him. It was a natural instinct. I'm sorry for what I did to your friend."

"His name was Luke." I corrected him.

"Chris," Rachel tried to calm me down. "Just stop. Please don't do this."

"No," I ignored her continuing to glare at Logan trying to make him feel weak and guilty. "You shot him twice. Why did you shoot him twice? Was that a natural instinct?"

"God dammit!" Logan slammed his fist onto the table making the bowls shake and making Rachel jump. I wasn't scared of him anymore.

"I just want to know why you shot Luke two times." I slammed my fist onto the table. "Why did you shoot him if he had already been shot? Was it your plan to take him out of the picture—"

"It was your plan to attack me!" Logan stood up and pointed his finger at me. His voice became monstrous. "It was you who attacked me! It was y—"

"Well," I stood up raising my voice. "It was you who kidnapped us, you fucking psycho!"

"Sit your ass down boy!" Logan roared. "I will not let any kids take control of me in my house that I built! Don't call me a psycho! I'm not a psycho!"

"Chris just sit down." Rachel demanded of me.

I looked at her and realized that I need to stop letting this anger take over before someone gets hurt. I sat down and calmed my self down.

Logan continued to stand up. He breathed heavily. He had a frown on his face.

I looked up at him then back at my food. I looked at Rachel who stared down at her bowl of cereal. That's when I had a plan that could actually work come to mind. It would take time but it would get Rachel and I out of here.

Logan wants respect and power over us. He wants authority in his household. Then I'll give him what he wants.

CHAPTER 13

We were, again, back in the room. Logan had put us in here after breakfast and told us that he'll come back for lunch.

Rachel was sitting on the bed staring at me with her dry eyes. "You can't do that shit anymore. You can't let your anger take over again." She paused for a moment and looked at the door. "He could've done something to you."

"I know," I said. "I'm sorry." I stared at the floor not making eye contact with her.

"What are we gonna do, Chris?" Rachel asked leaving the topic.

I wanted to tell her my plan but I couldn't. If I wanted this to work, I needed it to be genuine. She couldn't know and I need her to have real reactions to what I will eventually do.

"I don't know." I lied to her. It hurt me to lie to my best friend. I tell her everything but I can't tell her this. "We should just give up."

"What!" she hissed at me.

"We can't do anything, Rachel." I had to make this plan work. "We should just stop fighting and just live with the fact that we're not getting out of here."

"Are you okay, Chris?" Rachel looked at me like I was crazy. "What the hell are you talking about?"

"Rachel," I continued to not look at her. "You read in that journal about Connor and the others. You saw what happened to Luke. We can't do anything." I looked at her now in her eyes. I saw that she was confused. "We can't do anything, alright."

"Luke wouldn't do this." Rachel jabbed. "He would fight."

"Luke's not here, Rachel." I quickly responded back. She looked like she had been hurt by the comment. I hated this. I hated lying to her. "Fighting is what will get us killed." I was hoping that Logan was listening at the door. "Look, he may have kidnapped us but he is still feeding us and making sure we are okay. He is—"

"Chris, you sound crazy." she looked at me with even more confusion. "He killed Luke! He is a murderer and you just want to give up and relax with this psycho?" Rachel stepped up to me. Her eyes locked with mine. "Are you okay?"

"Yes." I wanted to tell her what I was trying to do but I couldn't. My plan is starting to work and I can't pussy out now. "Luke is dead and that is that." I couldn't believe that I just said that.

"*That is that?*" she repeated my words with anger. "You're insane, Chris." She took a few steps back. "He's your best friend."

"*Was* my best friend." I corrected her. I wanted to punch myself for saying that. Why would I say that?

Rachel walked up to me and slapped me as hard as she could to put some sense into me.

"What the hell, Rach?" I said placing my hand on the sting.

"Don't you ever say that!" she snapped in a demanding manner. "He *is* your best friend. He *is our* best friend. How could you ever say that?" Her eyes had raging fire in them but then the fire started to die down when the water started to fill and drop from her eyes. "This isn't you, Chris." Rachel wiped a tear from her cheek. "I don't know what's gotten into you but I need you. You're all I got and I can't lose you either."

I wanted to hug her but I couldn't do that. I just stood there looking at her with no emotion and she walked back to the bed and laid down facing away from me.

I could not believe that I said all that. I deserved to get slapped, I deserved a lot worse. She has no one but me and I'm being a jerk to her. But it's the only thing I can do in order for us to escape. I need to make it seem like I wanted to stay here with Logan and make him trust me. I needed to give him what he wanted so that I could get what I wanted.

What I'm doing to Rachel is just the first part of my idea and the rest is just to sweeten Logan up and make him feel comfortable so that, hopefully soon, I could strike.

It was now lunch and we sat at the table. Rachel didn't touch her food. She just sat there staring at it and sometimes would glance at me with a glare. I could see Logan, in the corner of my eye, staring at her.

"Rachel, you should eat." I advised her as I quickly glanced at Logan to see his reaction. "Logan made this food for us. Don't let it go to waste."

"I'm not hungry." Rachel looked at me in disgust. "And why would I let—"

"She is being ungrateful, Logan." I acted like I was trying to make Logan happy. "I'm sorry for the way she is acting."

"You trying to be funny, boy?" Logan looked at me weird. "Cause I'm not laughing."

"No." I lied to him. "I'm just saying, why fight something we can't beat. I mean...you are feeding us and giving us shelter." I continued my act hoping he wouldn't catch on. He's already suspicious but I can change that. "Let's talk about something else—"

"No." Logan mumbled. "I'm not stupid, kid. I'm not falling for your shit lies." His voice became stern. "You never talked this much before and now you do after what I did.

"Yeah," I looked at my plate no longer looking at Logan. "You're right. I'm sorry for trying to make this work."

Rachel looked at me in confusion. She looked like she was trying to figure me out.

"*Trying to make this work?*" Rachel repeated my words. "Are you serious right now, Chris?" She raised her voice.

"Now she's talking too." Logan said. "What's wrong with you two."

"Nothing's wrong with me." Rachel retorted. "But there's something wrong with you and him." She pointed at me. "Now I'm stuck in this place with two psychos."

"Watch it, girl." Logan ordered.

"Rachel just calm down." I was actually trying to caution her to keep her safe from Logan's oncoming wrath. If only she knew my plan.

"Shut the hell up, Chris." Rachel was now furious. "I don't know what's up with you, Chris. You're scaring me and you're making me mad."

"I'm sorry, Rachel." I apologized.

Rachel just sat there staring at me trying to figure out what was wrong with me. I wanted to tell her everything but that would ruin everything that I have planned.

"Can I please go back to the room." Rachel asked Logan while she continued to glare at me. "I'm not hungry and I don't wanna be here with you guys."

"Alright." Logan was now confused. He got up from his seat and walked her out of the dining room.

I was now alone in the dining room. I turned to my right to look at the floor where Luke had died. I fought back the tears that were trying to push their way out.

What am I doing? Why am I doing this to her? I began to question myself more and more wondering if this was actually going to work. Logan doesn't trust me and he won't let his guard down after the stunts we pulled.

I heard the door in the hallway open and then shut followed by Logan locking it.

"Hurry up and finish." he demanded as he came back into the dining room.

I did as I was told rushing to finish my sandwich. I gulped down my water as soon as I swallowed the last of the sandwich. I looked over to Logan, who was waiting in the dining room opening with his arms crossed. I looked at his shoulder remembering that Luke had stabbed him with the knife.

"Is your shoulder okay?" I asked as I got up from my seat.

"Just come on." he grunted turning around beginning to walk.

I followed him down the hallway. "Tell me about the journal." I blurted out trying to think of something to make him stop. "About Connor. What happened to him?"

Logan stopped in the middle of the hallway. He didn't turn around to face me. He just stood there breathing like a tired grizzly bear.

After a short moment, Logan had continued to the door, ignoring my question. He unlocked the door and opened it. I reluctantly walked into the room where Rachel sat at the bed, staring at the velvet carpet.

"Don't mention that name again." Logan mumbled as he close the door, gently this time. He locked it leaving me and Rachel in the room.

"I'm sorry." I said to her actually meaning it.

She didn't respond. She continued to stare at the floor. Her brown hair covered most of her face. Her arms crossed.

I wanted to go to her and hold her in my arms. That's what she needed. She needed me. She needed her best friend.

"Rachel," I began to walk to her but then I stopped myself knowing that this would cause my plan to fail.

This plan felt stupid. It was unnecessary to not tell her but it was the only way to make everything seem real to Logan. It would make our relationship seem destroyed and make him trust me more.

I want to tell her but I can't.

CHAPTER 14

Rachel and I sat in the room without sharing a word for long time. I assumed that it had been a couple hours, almost time for dinner.

Rachel got up from the bed and walked to the door. She quickly glanced at me with a glare. She banged on the door couple of times then waited.

I heard heavy footsteps come near the door. "What?" Logan calmly said behind the door.

"I have to go to the bathroom." Rachel replied in an annoyed tone.

"Dinner is almost done," Logan replied back. "Can you wait a few minutes?"

"No!" Rachel yelled. "It's an emergency!"

There was a sigh that came from outside the door. "Alright." Logan began unlocking the door. The door opened.

I stood up from where I was sitting. Logan stood there looking at me and Rachel.

"Go sit at the table, Chris." Logan told me. "Come on." Logan and Rachel walked down the hallway as I walked out of the room. I made my way towards the dining room and sat at the table as I was directed.

"Are you just gonna stand there and watch me?" Rachel's voice could be heard down the hall faintly.

"I don't want you kids to try any shit again." Logan quickly responded. "I don't trust you or him. So just go and do your business." Logan's voice became more agitated.

I sat there in the dining room looking around. I was going to go and check out the kitchen to see if I could find anything but I decided to play it safe.

A few minutes had past. Rachel and Logan walked into the kitchen. She sat down across from me and he went into the kitchen. She didn't look at me and I didn't look at her.

"What are you making?" I asked turning my head to face the kitchen.

"Fish and grits." Logan answered as I started to smell grits.

"Never had it." I lied to him. My mom used to make it for me and Caleb every once in a while. "I mean I never had them together."

"Well," Logan came into the dining room with two plates of food placing them in front of Rachel and I. "Hope you enjoy it." Logan flashed a faint smile that quickly faded away.

I took a piece of the fish and mixed it with some grits taking a bite out of it. "It's good." I smiled at Logan. I glanced at Rachel and she looked back at me with disgust.

"I'm glad you like it." Logan said as he sat in his seat.

"It makes sense why people put these together." I chuckled as I took another bite.

"Yep," Logan began to smile. "It's just like chicken and waffles."

"Exactly." I could sense him becoming more comfortable with me.

"Two different things together don't look good to others but they end up making something great." Logan grinned. "You two need a drink?"

"Yes, please." I responded.

Logan got up from his seat and made his way into the kitchen.

"What the hell are you doing?" Rachel whispered as silently as possible.

My smile faded away and I shook my head slowly trying to give her a sign.

"You like Kool-aid?" Logan came into the room handing us the drinks.

"Yes." I brought my fake smile back. "Thank you." I took a sip of my drink looking at Rachel then looking back at Logan.

"This is really good." Rachel admired Logan's dinner. I knew she was faking. She flashed her teeth and looked at me quickly as if she either was trying to mock me or she knew what I was doing.

"That's good." Logan sat down. His grin becoming bigger. "Have you had it before?"

"Yes," Rachel declared. She giggled as she drank her Kool-aid. "My dad use to make it for me when I was a kid." She started to chuckle and her chuckles became laughter. She started to cough still laughing.

I looked at her with caution wondering if she was okay.

"You okay?" Logan started to nervously laugh with her.

Rachel grabbed for her drink and drank some. She swallowed it and placed her hand on her chest. She laughed even more. "I'm sorry but I was just thinking of the time when I tried making this. It was like a year ago and I wanted to make some for myself because my parents were out of town." Rachel gained control of herself. "So, I tried making fish and grits and I'm looking up how to fry the fish, right, and I was doing fine with the grits but the fish was the hard part. So, I do all the stuff for the fish and put it in the pan." Rachel started to giggle. "The fish was frying and then suddenly out of nowhere the thing starts catching on fire." Rachel starts laughing harder.

"What!" Logan laughed with her. "What did you do?"

"Oh my god!" Rachel continued laughing. "I started panicking and lost my shit. I was screaming at the fish and yelling for help. The smoke alarm was going off. All hell was in my kitchen. So then I called Luke." Rachel's laugh and grin started to vanish. Logan's did as well and I continued looking at her with concern. "He came over and he helped me and we just ended up eating the grits and we laughed about it all night. He helped me clean everything up and we just spent time together." Rachel's eyes started to well with tears. "That's the night I remember every time I think of him because that's when we became close." Rachel glared at Logan directly in the eyes making his smile vanish for good. Then she looked at me.

"Rachel," I cautioned her. She was ruining my plan. "Don't d—"

"I'm not gonna do anything, Chris." she quickly retorted. "I just wanted to remind you that this man, this monster took away our friend. Trying to make sure that you are still right in the head."

My eyes started to fill with tears. I was mad at myself for what I was about to do. "Luke's death was your fault." I felt the tears slowly slide down my cheeks.

There was a moment of silence. Logan looked at me in confusion. Rachel stared at me in shock. The silence filled the room completely and I could feel the guilt eat away at my insides.

"Wh-what?" Rachel forced herself to speak. Her eyes let out the tears and she began to sniffle.

"You were the one..." I couldn't finish my sentence. I tried holding back my tears from rushing out. "You were the one who took the knife and brought it to the room." I had to make this plan carry out perfectly.

"How could you say that?" she sniffled. "How dare you."

"I tried to tell you guys that we needed to play if safe." I was hurt and felt sick for what I was saying. "If you didn't bring that knife into that room, then he would probably still be alive."

"Uh," Logan cleared his voice. "Do you want to go to the room?" Logan asked Rachel.

She stood up without speaking and walked out of the dining room. Logan looked at me as he got up and then followed her out.

I was all alone in the dining room again. I put my face in my hands and started sobbing. I didn't mean any of what I said.

After Logan had put her in the room, he came walking into the dining room. He sat at the table with me as I cried.

"Maybe you should wait it out for a bit before you go back." Logan sighed.

We just sat there and I kept on crying not knowing what to do. Logan was the one who killed Luke. It was his fault and I made it seem like it was hers.

"It's okay," Logan rested his hand on my shoulder. I wanted to move away from this beast but I couldn't do it if I wanted to get me and Rachel out of here.

CHAPTER 15

Logan walked me out of the dining room to the secret door and opened it. I saw that Rachel was asleep on the bed. It had been an hour since the whole situation had happened.

I walked in as Logan closed the door behind me and locked it. I walked over to Rachel's resting body and placed my hand on her arm.

"I'm sorry." I whispered as I removed my hand and walked to the other sided of the room laying down on the floor. I laid there staring at the ceiling wondering what my mom and Albert and Joanna were doing. Were they looking for me? Of course they were.

I felt bad for what I had said to her and I wanted to wake her to tell her everything but she had to rest.

I began to feel tired and my eyes began to feel heavy then they closed and I drifted off.

I was in a room on my knees. The room was dark, almost pitch black but there was a light illuminating me. I stood up and looked around me to see nothing but darkness. I tried stepping out of the light into the darkness but I couldn't leave the circle of light.

"Hello?" I called out.

There was no response. The darkness and silence of the room was making me feel unsettled.

"Chris." a whisper came from behind me.

I turned around to the voice. My hairs on my arms and neck raised as I saw a dark figure standing in the darkness. It looked like a human but it had two large horns coming from their head.

"Who are you?" I asked.

The figure just stood there staring at me. Then, there were two dark, yellow eyes that had pupils like a snake.

"Don't look at him." a familiar voice came from next to me.

I turned to see my mom step out from the darkness revealing herself. She was wearing a white dress and white heels.

"Mom." I tried to step out of the light to grab her but I was still stuck. It was as if something was blocking me like some type of force field. "Mom, please help me." I placed my hands on the force field.

"It's okay, baby." she gently smiled at me. "Don't worry. This is just your punishment for what you did." My mom continued to smile but there were tears falling from her eyes.

"Mom," I was confused with what was happening. "What are you talking about?"

"Why weren't you there for him!" her voice became deep. "You let my boy die! Caleb! Caleb! Caleb!" My mom wept as she fell to her knees. "My baby! You let him die! Why! Why my baby, Lord!"

"Mommy!" I cried out. "Mommy please stop it! Don't say that! I wanted to be there for him!"

"I hate you!" she screamed as she slid back into the darkness as if she was yanked by something.

"Mom!" I screamed slamming the invisible force field that blocked me from the outside. "Mom!"

"Chris," Luke's voice came from the opposite side.

I quickly turned around to face him as he stepped out from the darkness. He had blood spewing out from his chest and his neck. There was a little blood dripping from his mouth.

"I wish you had stayed with me." Luke sounded calm. There were tears welling up in his eyes.

"Don't do this to me, Luke." I fell to my knees putting my face in my hands. "Don't blame me." I sobbed wanting to wake up from this nightmare.

"Get out of here!" I heard Caleb's voice. I looked up to see him standing there looking behind me. "Leave him alone!" Caleb continued to scream at the darkness.

I turned around to see the yellow eyes that were originally staring at me before. This time it revealed itself in the light just a little. It's body was of a dirty, red color and it had no clothing. It's body was covered in scars. It was carrying a large pitchfork.

At it's feet was Logan. He was holding onto the being's leg tightly. He stared at me with terror and he wouldn't let go of his stare.

"Logan?" I stood back up and looked down at him.

He didn't respond. He just continued to look at me with fear in his eyes. He looked up at the creature and started crying. The creature pointed it's pitchfork at me slowly.

I looked down at my hands and I was suddenly carrying the rifle that I had threaten Logan with before. I couldn't let go of it and I could feel my grip get tighter and I felt like I had no control of my body as I began to aim the gun at Logan.

Then, there was screaming. I was now illuminated by a red light and I quickly looked around me to see Luke and Caleb inflamed in fire. They screamed my name as their skin started to melt off of their bodies. I looked back at Logan and the creature to see that the creature was now taller. It's face was now revealed to me and it was horrifying. I screamed at the terrifying creature as it smirked at me with it's sharp, rotting teeth.

"Chris!" Rachel's voice called out to me.

I continued to scream in terror at the creature feeling petrified and trapped in my position. I wanted to move the gun up to aim it at the creature but I couldn't move it away from Logan who was now crying louder than before.

"Please!" Logan cried out to me as if he was begging to me. "Please!" Logan yelled out to me.

There was now fire everywhere. It illuminated the whole room and it was the room that Logan had trapped us in. I could see my mom, Joanna, Luke, and Caleb all in the fire burning and screaming.

"Do it, Chris!" Rachel's voice was heard and it sounded louder. "Do it!" Her voice took over the room but she was no where in the room.

I could now see the creature in full form. It was more horrifying then before. It's horns were now protruding out of the ceiling. It was now muscular and it's body was glistening with sweat from the heat of the fire.

It reminded me of a demon or some type of devil. I was scared of what I was looking at and I didn't know what to do.

"Chris!" Rachel screamed my name repeatedly. Every time she called my name it got louder and louder until it became deafening.

"Help me!" I wept as my finger pressed on the trigger. "Please! Please! Someone please help me!"

I was awoken by the knocking of the door.

"You guys up?" Logan's voice asked from outside.

"Uh," I drowsily arose from my nightmare. I looked over to Rachel. She was sitting at the bed and reading the journal that Connor had written in. "Yeah, we're up." I rubbed my eyes as I yawned. I stood up and stretched.

Logan opened the door after unlocking it. I walked out of the room. Logan stood there staring at Rachel as she continued to sit at the bed reading the journal.

"Where did you find that?" Logan seemed a little concerned. He took a step into the room.

"He found it." Rachel glared at me.

"Give it to me." Logan demanded as he walked up to Rachel snatching the journal from her. "Get up. Breakfast is ready."

"I'm not hungry." Rachel frowned at Logan then she looked at me. "I don't want to waste your food."

Logan stood there for a moment. "Okay." he sighed as he walked out of the room closing it and then locking it. "You're hungry, right?" Logan asked me as we began to walk to the dining room.

"Yes." I answered. "What's for breakfast?" I asked as we made it into the dinging room. I sat at the table feeling nervous for some reason.

"Eggs and bacon." Logan went into the kitchen. He came back with two plates and placed them in front of me and in front of his seat.

"You're eating?" I knew that was a dumb question to ask.

"Might as well." he answered as he sat down in his seat.

We sat there eating our breakfast in silence. I kept thinking about the dream I had last night. It was confusing and made me wonder what the whole meaning was.

Logan finished his food after a couple of minutes and went into the kitchen to clean the plate. He came back in and sat back down with me as I was getting ready to finish my breakfast.

"How long did you know?" Logan asked as he placed Connor's journal on the table.

"Oh...uh," I swallowed my food and cleared my throat. "I found it a few days ago. The day before Luke..." I couldn't get the words out.

Logan sighed as he grabbed his drink and sipped it. "Everything in there is true. I'm sorry you guys had to find out like this."

I looked at him and then at the journal. I watched as he stared at the journal. He looked sad and he looked like he was reflecting on things. I almost felt bad for him knowing that he had some type of emotion and regret in him.

"I needed them," Logan began to speak again. "I needed them and I just took their lives away."

"Needed them?" I questioned him. What did he need from these kids? What did he need from us?

Logan looked up from the journal to me. "Nothing. It's nothing."

We sat there in long silence. I wonder why he needed them. Why would he need to kidnap kids and hold them hostage?

"Here." Logan slid the journal over to me.

"Why?" I asked as I held the journal in hand.

"Well, you guys are gonna be bored and I wanna give y'all something to do." Logan replied as he got up from his seat starting towards the kitchen. He returned back into the dining room and handed me a pen.

"Thanks." I took the pen and placed it inside the journal.

"No problem." Logan smiled a little. "You done with your food?"

I nodded. Logan took my plate and went back into the kitchen. I sat there and stared at the journal. I began to flip through it realizing that there were dates.

"You ready to go back?" Logan asked as he came back in.

"Yeah," I stood up and began to walk then stopped to turn around. "Hey, what's the date?"

"Today is...uh," Logan looked into the kitchen which I assume he was doing because there was a calendar. "It's October 29th." Logan answered.

"Thanks." I quickly wrote down the date on an empty page of the journal. I closed the journal as me and Logan made our way to the secret door.

CHAPTER 16

10/29/18

Just came back from breakfast with Logan. Not sure what to write in this. When I spoke to Logan this morning, he was about to tell me something but changed the subject. He said that he needed Connor and the others. I didn't know what he meant by that but I'm going to find out. It seems that he is beginning to trust me and maybe there is a more likely chance that me and Rachel will get out of here. Rachel hasn't spoken to me since I returned back to the room. She hates me right now because of my plan. She thinks that I am trying to kiss Logan's ass but I'm really trying to get him to trust me so that I can get us out. There is this weird tension between us and it makes me feel bad especially after Luke's death. I still can't believe that he is gone. I can't think of him right now and I need to focus on my plan and getting me and Rachel the hell out of here.

10/30/18

Nothing really crazy has happened. Had lunch and dinner yesterday. Rachel didn't come for both and continued to stay in the room. I managed to convince Logan to let me bring her back some food. This morning she came to breakfast but she didn't talk. She still hasn't talked to me and I understand why. I know she feels alone in this place and I feel bad for her. She also came to lunch but she skipped dinner. So at dinner it was just me and Logan. We talked and we laughed. He is warming up to me and that means that my plan is working.

11/1/18

Just woke up from a bad dream. It was one of the scariest dreams I've had. I saw Rachel chained to a door and Logan was beating her with a belt. He wouldn't stop and I wanted to do something but I couldn't move. She kept screaming and I wanted it all to stop. Then, Luke showed up and started yelling at me and he kept saying that it was my fault. I was crying and everything felt terrible. I don't know why I'm writing in this journal but I guess it gives me something to do. I didn't write yesterday. I really didn't have anything to share. Tomorrow I'm going to see if I can manage to get Logan to tell me anything and try to get him to trust me.

11/2/18

This morning we were all at the table. Rachel didn't talk. She just looked angrily at me and Logan as we talked. Logan told some jokes and I faked laughed. Then at lunch, it was just me and Logan. We talked, laughed, ate, etc. Then, there was dinner. Rachel didn't want to come to dinner but Logan forced her to come. After we got done with dinner we played Logan's favorite card game, Blackjack. In the first couple of games, everything was fine and normal. Rachel didn't know how to play and so she watched Logan and I demonstrate the rules to her for the first game. Logan won the first few games and he was happy and all. Then that's when Rachel had won one of the games. Logan got mad and slammed his fist on the table. Rachel raised her voice at him and told him to relax and that it was just a game. Then they started to argue and Rachel was not giving up. So, I tried to calm Logan down and I told Rachel to shut up. This made her mad but I managed to somehow calm her down as well. I just didn't understand how people can get mad at losing a game of Blackjack. I mean Logan won more games then Rachel and she won and he loses his shit. He's a psycho. Anyways, after the argument had settled down, Logan called Rachel an ungrateful bitch. Rachel didn't take it so easily and that's when Rachel jumped out of her seat and threw a punch at Logan's nose. Logan quickly got up and it didn't even look like Rachel's hit hurt. He put his hands around her neck and pushed her against the wall. My first instinct was to go and save her but I ignored that instinct to stick to my plan. So I stood up calmly and told Logan to let her go. He looked really scary and I didn't want him to hurt her but I couldn't make him lose trust in me. Logan started yelling in her face that she was ungrateful and that she should respect him. That's when I saw him reach for his gun and I quickly screamed at him that he needed us. I told him that he needed us because that's when I remembered that he said that he needed Connor and those other girls. Logan still had his hand on his gun and his other squeezing Rachel's neck. I kept telling him that he needed us and that he couldn't kill us. I told him to give her another chance. To my surprise, he listened. Logan threw Rachel to the ground. She wasn't crying and she seemed to be ready to die. Before she could even get up, Logan grabbed her hair and dragged her to the secret room. I stood there shocked and afraid of this man. Logan came and got me without saying a word and he took me to the secret room. Rachel and I didn't speak to each other but she did tell me 'thank you'. Now I know that Logan definitely does need us for something. He can't hurt us if I keep reminding him that he needs us. I just need to know what for.

11/6/18

Didn't write for the past four days. We just did the same stuff everyday. We played different card games and board games after dinner. Rachel didn't play at all and she just watched. Logan didn't even look at her and he seemed to be still angry at her. I guess you could say that me and Logan had a "good time". I mean Logan had a good time, I'm just acting like I did too. I did, however, enjoy beating Logan in a couple of games. Logan sucked at Uno and I destroyed them in it all the time. Logan didn't get mad at me when I won though. He just laughed and would just move on to the next round or game. Today we did the same thing. We had breakfast, lunch, and dinner and then we played games. He gave me and Rachel the card game, Uno, to play when we are bored. Nothing really special has happened but I just felt like writing to pass the time and fall asleep.

CHAPTER 17

Rachel and I sat on opposite sides of the room. She sat on the bed and I sat on the floor next to the door. I was shuffling cards that Logan had just given us.

"Wanna play?" I asked Rachel. I wanted to make her feel better and make her feel like she wasn't alone. She needed me.

"Sure." Rachel reluctantly answered as she moved from the bed to the floor where I was sitting.

I smiled at her as she came over. I started shuffling the cards again and put seven cards out. I flipped the card from the deck over and the game started.

"What does Logan need us for?" Rachel asked placing the card down. She was talking about the other night when hell broke loose.

"I don't know." I honestly really didn't know what he needed us for. I placed one of my cards down. "He told me that he needed Connor and Annie and Julia."

"What the hell?" Rachel pulled from the deck until she had the right card. "So he's telling you all his secrets?" Rachel sounded a little angry.

"No," I placed another card down. "We just talked."

"What are you trying to do, Chris?" Rachel tilted her head and squinted her eyes.

"Nothing, Rach." I lied to her. "It's your turn." I looked down at the cards.

"You're lying." Rachel declared.

"No I'm not." I said in a calm voice. "Logan's giving us a place to live and he's trying—"

"Shut the hell up, Chris!" Rachel hissed as she threw her cards down. "That's how I know. This guy killed your best friend! He killed our best friend! You keep saying the same thing!" She stood up and looked down at me. "He kidnapped us, Chris! We are not getting out of here unless we work together!"

"Well we tried that before." I grabbed the cards and put them all back together. "And that got one of us killed. You were almost gonna be killed, Rachel." I kept my voice quiet. "Logan is giving us resources and he's not letting us starve to death."

"It doesn't matter!" Rachel argued. "I want to get home and see my family! You're acting like you don't wanna leave this place and you're acting like you don't care about Luke. I don't know what's wrong with you but Im getting out of this place. I'm getting out of here tomorrow!"

"Rachel!" I stood up and grabbed her arms. I had to tell her everything. "I don't want to be here. I want to get the hell out of here. Listen to me. Just listen to me, please." I couldn't lie to her any longer and if I didn't do anything she would've ended up hurt or dead. "This is all a part of my plan"

"What?" Rachel asked.

"I've been acting like this because Im trying to get us out of here." I sat her down on the bed. I made sure that my voice was quiet.

"How does that make any since?" Rachel was confused.

"Because, Rachel, I had to make Logan trust me." I continued on. "I've been trying to get him to trust me so that I can get him to tell me what his purpose for this is and let him trust me enough to the point where I can attack him and get us out of here."

"This doesn't make any sense, Chris." Rachel looked at me almost feeling relieved but still shocked. "You had to get him to trust you for what?"

"So I could catch him off guard." I explained. "It made sense in my head but I gotta learn more about this guy. He's starting to trust me and I can get him to tell me everything. You just gotta wait until the time is right. You have to keep acting like you've been acting. I'm sorry Rachel but this is gonna work if we just do it right."

"Okay, okay." Rachel looked at me with hope. "It's okay."

"I didn't mean anything that I said to you." I confessed. "I didn't mean any of it."

"I know." Rachel put her hand in my mine. "Just get us out of here."

"I am." I told her. "We're gonna get out of here."

CHAPTER 18

It was now lunchtime. Rachel didn't come and so it was just me and Logan.

"So you got any siblings, Chris?" Logan asked as he ate a fry.

"Yep." I told Logan. Then that's when I realized that I could make Logan feel empathy for me. "I have an older sister and I use to have a younger brother." I knew it was wrong to use my dead brother for sympathy but I needed Logan to trust me.

"Oh no," Logan looked sad. "I'm sorry. When did he—"

"Last year." my eyes started to become watery and my vision became blurred. I didn't like talking about my brother and I couldn't believe that I was telling a psychopath about him. "He committed suicide. It was an overdose." I wiped my tears on my arms.

"Wow." Logan seemed to actually feel emotional. "What was his name?"

"His name was Caleb." I told Logan. "Anyways, enough of that. Tell me about your life." I smiled as I continued to wipe the tears away. "You got any siblings?"

"Yeah," Logan looked at me. "I had two older sisters and an older brother."

"You were close with them?" I asked.

"Not really." Logan answered as he took a sip of his drink. "I didn't really talk to them or hang out with them. I was more closer to Zoe more than anybody in my family."

"Who?" I quickly asked. I was learning more about him. "Who is Zoe?"

"She was my girlfriend in high school." Logan seemed to trust me and he was spilling everything onto me.

"What was she like?" I continued to question him more.

"She was beautiful." Logan shared. "Zoe was one of the nicest girls in that school. She was smart and funny and she was kind. I loved her so much."

"What happened to her?" I took a bite out of my hotdog.

"Her family made her stop seeing me. They made her go to a different school and everything." Logan looked like he was about to cry.

"Why would they do that?" I asked him trying to get more out of him.

"Because," Logan looked at me and then realized he was telling me things he didn't want me to know. "You know I shouldn't be telling you this."

"No," I had to keep him going. "I won't tell anyone."

"Why should I tell you?" Logan seemed to be onto me.

"I don't know." I began to do my act. "I haven't really had any conversations with anyone. Rachel won't talk to me. I want to get to know more about you. But it's fine if you don't feel comfortable telling me."

"It's fine." Logan smiled at me. "Feels good to talk to someone."

"Yeah, me too." I lied.

"Zoe was the only black girl in our school." Logan went back to his past. "No one liked her because she was black. I was the only one that saw the beauty in her. We walked together every morning to school, because we only lived a few minutes away from each other." Logan ate another fry. "I was her only friend and she was my only friend. We were together all the time. You couldn't separate us and we loved each other. Then, one day after a couple of months of dating, she told me she was pregnant. Now, in high school, being pregnant is basically a sin. Also at our high school, in our time, having a mixed baby was a sin also. Me and Zoe were the only ones that were excited about this baby. I didn't care about our skin color but our families did." Logan took a bite out of his hotdog and swallowed. "My family and her family hated each other. My racist family made Zoe get an abortion. They took our baby away from us." Logan had a tear slide down his cheek. "Then her family took her away from me. I haven't seen or heard from Zoe in thirty years."

"I'm sorry, Logan." I genuinely felt sorry for him. I wasn't acting.

"It's fine." Logan cleared his throat. "But that's why I need you and Rachel."

"What?" I asked. The room was dead silent and the only sound that was heard was the ticking of the clock form the hallway. "What do you mean?"

"I need you and Rachel." Logan said.

"I know what you said but why?" I was about to find out his main purpose for kidnapping us.

"You're black and she is white." Logan said in a calm voice as he took another sip of his drink.

"What?" I knew what he said and I was hoping I misheard him.

"You and Rachel are going to have my baby." Logan told me.

"Yo-you want...you want me and Rachel to..." I couldn't even speak. I was shocked.

"That's why I needed Connor and Annie but Annie wasn't complying so I took Julia." Logan told me in the most unsettling manner. "They were both black girls and Connor was white. I saw you and Rachel at the gas station and I saw that you guys had a relationship. I knew that you two would be perfect."

"Bu-but why did you take Luke?" I asked as tears started to come again. "Luke is white and you didn't need him."

"I couldn't leave him in that car." Logan continued. "He was in the way though but I wasn't planning on killing him because he was your friend but you guys kept trying to escape."

"Why didn't you just let him go? You could've let him go." I sniffled as more tears came rushing down.

"Chris, I'm sorry." Logan ate another fry. "All I'm asking for is a baby from you two."

"And will you let us go?" I asked trying to maintain myself.

"Chris, you know I can't do that." Logan took the last bite of his hotdog.

"What are you gonna do with us after?" I couldn't even see his face now.

"I'm gonna kill you." Logan said the words so calm that it made my whole body shiver. "Don't cry, Chris. If it's a boy, I'll name him Caleb or Chris. Which ever you prefer."

I wiped my tears and got clear view of him. This man was going to kill us no matter what. He's a maniac, a psychopath, a killer.

"But since Rachel is not really complying." Logan went on. "I guess I'll have to get rid of her and find a new—"

"No!" I raised my voice. "No, please don't. You don't have to kill her, Logan. She's just getting used to you. That's all."

"Okay." Logan said. "Make sure she's on board with this when you go back to the room. Then at dinner we can all talk about it."

"Yep." I tried to stay calm. "Okay."

CHAPTER 19

"He wants us to have his baby?" Rachel was shocked.

"Yeah." I paced back and forth in the small area of the room. "He said he is gonna kill us after the baby is born."

"What the hell, Chris." Rachel sat down on the bed. "He's gonna kill us."

"Don't worry." I said trying to calm her down. "Just act like you are okay with this when we go to dinner tonight."

"But I'm not." Rachel said.

"Rachel." I cautioned her. "Just do it."

"Okay." Rachel complied with me. "I'm sorry but this is freaking weird."

"I know." I sat down on the floor resting my head on the wall behind me. "He could've let Luke go, Rach."

"Was he gonna kill Luke no matter what?" Rachel looked at me.

"He said that he would've let him live." I told her. "He still killed him though. He's gonna pay for this."

We sat at the table in silence eating our dinner. Logan kept looking at me and Rachel. We didn't make eye contact with him. I felt sick and disgusted.

"Did you tell her?" Logan asked.

"He did." Rachel answered for me. She took a bite of her food "I think that it makes sense." Rachel lied.

"Really?" Logan was shocked.

"Yes." Rachel looked at me and then at Logan. "When do you want us to… you know…"

"Oh," Logan clapped and grinned. "You can do it anytime you want. When the time is right, go for it."

Rachel and I nodded awkwardly. We continued to eat. Then, an idea came to my mind.

"Hey, Logan." I placed my fork down and sipped some of my water. "Can we have pancakes for breakfast tomorrow?"

"Uh, sure." Logan looked confused. "Why pancakes?"

"They're good." I had an idea and I was going to act on it. "We haven't had them since—"

"Yeah, I know." Logan interrupted trying to not be reminded of that day. "I'll make them extra special for you guys." Logan was happy.

"Thank you." I told him with a fake smile. I looked at Rachel and she looked at me with confusion. I'm going to tell her everything when we get back to the room.

Rachel and I sat on the bed next to each other staring at the wall.

"Why did you ask for pancakes?" Rachel asked still staring at the wall.

"Because I have a plan." I answered her.

"What the hell are pancakes gonna do?" she turned her head and looked at me.

"Last time he gave us butter knives to cut our pancakes." I explained. "So I plan on cutting myself with the knife."

"How are you gonna cut yourself with a butterknife?" Rachel questioned me.

"I've done it before." I told her. "I just need to put enough force onto my finger."

"Okay." Rachel decided to not question it anymore. "So what are you gonna do after that?"

"I'm gonna make him make another pancake and wait till it's on the pan." I continued on with my plan. "I'm gonna cut my finger and Logan will come running into the room and try to help me with the cut. I'm gonna keep his attention until the pancakes start to burn and smoke." I looked Rachel in the eyes. "Hopefully he tells you to go into the kitchen and do something with the burnt pancake. You're gonna grab the pan while I keep him distracted and then you'll come in and knock him in the head as hard as you can."

"Wait." Rachel stopped me. "What if he doesn't tell me go into the kitchen?"

"Then we go with option number two." I looked at the journal that was on the floor. "I'll use the pen on him when he's close enough and stab him in the throat. I'm gonna get the gun and keys and you run as fast you can to the door when I throw you the keys. I'll have the gun and I'll be right there with you protecting you while you unlock the door."

"Okay." Rachel nodded. "We can do this. We're gonna get out of here."

"We are." I looked back at the wall. "For Connor, for Annie, for Julia, and for Luke."

CHAPTER 20

It was morning. Rachel was asleep on the bed and I was awake sitting at the edge waiting for Logan to come to the door. I had been awake all night and couldn't get any sleep. I looked down at the journal that was on the floor. I walked over to it and grabbed it. I opened the journal and took the pen out of it. I began to write.

11/7/18

Today me and Rachel are getting out of this place. Logan told me that he needed us to have his baby. He's a psychopath and he's gonna pay for what he's done. We've got a plan and I'm sure it will work. I want to write in here just case we don't make it out alive. I'm writing to make sure that whoever reads this next gets out of here alive and tell our families about us and that we love them. Don't really have much to say but good luck.

There was a knock on the door. It was Logan and it was time for breakfast. I stuck the pen in my pocket and looked over to Rachel. She was already up. She looked at me with fear.

"You guys up?" Logan started to unlock the door.

"Yep." I answered as I stood up. I walked over to the mattress and slid the journal into it.

Logan opened the door. He had a huge grin on his face. "Made pancakes."

We sat at the table eating our pancakes. I made sure to eat mine fast. I stuffed my mouth with more and more pancakes and ate as if I hadn't eaten in years.

"You must love them pancakes, boy." Logan chuckled as he wiped his mouth with a napkin.

There were so many pancakes in my mouth, that I couldn't even speak. I nodded to him and did my usual fake smile. I swallowed the food and drank some water to wash the remains down.

I looked over to Rachel. She was eating her food slow and I could see that her hands were trembling. She was nervous. I was nervous too but there was no turning back now.

"You okay, darlin?" Logan saw that Rachel was trembling. "You're shaking."

"I'm fine." Rachel quickly answered exposing her nervousness even more. "I'm—I'm just a little chilly." Rachel grabbed her drink and sipped some of it down. "But I'll be fine though."

Logan didn't say anything. He just nodded. He looked at my plate, which was almost clean. I made sure to save a half of a pancake to cut it. "You want me to make some more?" Logan asked the question that I wanted to hear.

"Yes." I answered. "Yes, please."

Logan got up from the table and made his way into the kitchen. I turned around to see him place the batter onto the sizzling hot pan. I turned back around to look at Rachel. I nodded to her slowly and she nodded back. Then, I started to cut the pancake and placed my finger on the food and applied pressure. I started slicing my finger until there was a hot fluid gushing out. There was a sharp pain and that's when I started to scream.

"Shit!" I screamed as loud as I could. I grabbed my hand and acted like I was trying to stop the bleeding when I was really squeezing more blood out. "Shit! Logan! Logan my finger!"

"What!" Logan came rushing back into the dining room. "What happened!"

"I cut my finger!" I screamed loudly and tried to make it seem as real as possible.

"How did you do that?" Logan yelled at me in confusion as he grabbed my hand to stop the bleeding.

There was smoke filling the room and it was coming from the kitchen. I coughed as the smoke made it's way into my lungs. Rachel stood up.

"Shit!" Logan yelled as he looked at the kitchen. He looked at Rachel. "Go in there and put the pan in the sink and put some cold water on it!" Logan put pressure on my finger. He had my blood on his hands. "How did you cut yourself with a butterknife?"

I saw Rachel come into the room with the pan and she had it above and she swung down as hard as she could slamming the hot pan hard onto Logan's head. He didn't fall to the ground but he winced in pain. He turned around and Rachel raised the pan again and swung it down even harder connecting it with Logan's head. The second time he fell to the floor.

"You bastard!" Rachel roared as she slammed the pan over Logan's head again. "You psycho!" She slammed the pan on his head again and this time there was blood sliding down from his forehead to his chin.

"Rachel!" I grabbed her arm to calm her down. I got onto the floor and searched Logan for the keys and instead I found the gun. I found the keys next and grabbed them. I threw them to Rachel. "Go!"

We both ran out of the dining room and down the hallway. We made it to the door and Rachel quickly tried unlocking the locks. She unlocked the first two locks fast surprisingly. She struggled with the third lock and she started breathing fast. I turned around to aim the gun down the hallway.

"No!" Logan screamed from the dining room. "Come back!" He roared.

Rachel unlocked the third lock and she was now on the last one.

"You pieces of shits!" Logan came stumbling into the hallway. His face had stripes of blood. His knuckles were balled and he started coming closer to me and Rachel.

"Rachel, come on!" I hurried her up as Logan got closer. I had my finger on the trigger. "Stay back! Just stay back, Logan!" He continued to get closer. Then, Logan started running towards me. I pulled the trigger and there was a loud bang. I shot the gun but I missed Logan. He tackled me down and he knocked the gun out of my hand and he was now on top of me with his hands on my neck.

"You're not leaving me!" Logan growled as his hands squeezed my throat tighter and tighter.

The air was leaving my body. I tried to fight back and pull his hands off of me but he kept putting pressure on my neck. I gasped for air. I could hear Rachel scream but I knew she was still trying the lock. Then, I realized that I had something. I had the pen in my pocket.

"Fuck you!" I said with the air that was left. I grabbed the pen from my pocket and pulled it out. I raised the pen and stabbed Logan's eye. There was a squish sound and it was followed by the screams and whimpers of Logan. His grip released from my neck as he fell. I got up and grabbed the gun.

"Yes!" Rachel cheered as she unlocked the last lock. She turned the knob and pulled the door open.

There was an open yard and there were trees everywhere. The front yard was covered in grass and had little spots of dirt. There was a big red truck with a dent in the front of it. I guess that's what Logan had hit us with. It felt amazing to be outside and to breathe fresh air. Rachel and I just stood there for a moment taking it all in. But that was all short lived.

"The truck." I grabbed Rachel's arm and pulled her to the truck. She went into the driver's seat and I was in the passenger's seat.

"Come on, come on!" Rachel yelled as she rushed to turn on the truck. She kept trying the ignition and the truck finally started.

"Drive! Drive!" I couldn't wait to get the hell out of here. Rachel pulled the gear stick to all the way to drive instead of reverse. I quickly realized this. "Rachel wait! Wait!"

Rachel stepped on the gas pedal and we went speeding into the house. The truck crashed through the wooden house and into the dining room. There was glass everywhere and wood was all over the hood of the truck.

"You okay?" I asked Rachel as she put the gear shift in reverse and tried reversing the truck.

"Yeah." Rachel had blood on her temple. She didn't care. She was just trying to get out of this place. The truck groaned as Rachel tried to reverse it. The truck was stuck on something.

"Forget it!" I told Rachel as I tried to open the door on my side but it wouldn't open. The wood was blocking the door. "Shit! Shit!" I slammed my fist onto the dashboard of the truck. "My door! It's stuck!"

Rachel tried opening her door but it was also stuck. "I can't open it!" She kept trying to open the door but it wouldn't budge.

"Roll down the window!" I demanded her as there was a loud bang and glass exploded everywhere. I turned around to see, through the broken glass of the truck, Logan aiming the rifle, from the wall, at us. "Go! Go go go go!"

Rachel started rolling down the window and as soon as it went all the way down, she pulled herself out from the seat and managed to get out. She fell to the ground.

There was another loud bang. Logan had shot at me again but he missed again. I moved to the driver's seat and pulled myself out of the truck. I fell to the ground hard on my arm. I winced in pain and I was helped up by Rachel.

"Stop!" Logan shot the gun again at the truck. We hid behind the truck for cover. "You're not leaving!"

I grabbed the gun from my pocket and stood up and shot at Logan. I hit his shoulder where Luke had previously stabbed him. Logan collapsed to the ground and grabbed at his shoulder.

I ran over to him and grabbed the rifle from him. He started crawling to his truck. When he made it, he rested his body on the tire of the truck. He still had the pen that I stabbed him with in the eye. He was still holding his wound on his shoulder and there was blood seeping through his clothes. He was breathing heavily.

"Why?" I aimed the rifle down at Logan's head. Rachel came from behind the truck and ran towards me. She stood next to me. "Why did you kill those kids?"

"Because." Logan had blood all over his face. His hair was drenched in sweat.

"Because what!" I continued to aim at Logan.

"Because I wanted my baby." Logan mumbled. He said a few words under his breath but I couldn't make out what he was saying. He started to cough up some blood. He then started to cry.

"Chris, let's go!" Rachel yelled at me.

"Just kill me already!" Logan screamed and then he winced in pain. "Do it! Just do it! There's bullets this time! So go ahead and get it over with." Logan demanded as he spit blood onto the ground.

I didn't know what to do. I had a gun to this man's face and he was helpless. Would I avenge Luke? Would I avenge the families of all those kids that were killed by this man? Was I going to let this man live and let him rot in prison or was I going to kill this man and let him rot in hell? I don't want to be a killer but I also don't want to let this monster walk the earth. Do I kill him? Do I let him live? What would you do?